Snowed Inn For Christmas

Samantha Baca

Cover Design: Jack'd Up Book Covers

<u>Silver Falls Duet</u>

Snowed Inn For Christmas

Murder and Mistletoe

Content Warning

Stalking

Kidnapping (of child)

Violence and foul language

Sexual content

Contents

One	1
Two	7
Three	13
Four	19
Five	31
Six	37
Seven	45
Eight	51
Nine	53
Ten	59
Eleven	65
Twelve	69
Thirteen	73
Fourteen	79
Fifteen	85
Sixteen	93
Seventeen	95
Eighteen	101
Nineteen	107
Twenty	111
Twenty One	115
Twenty Two	123
Twenty Three	129
Twenty Four	135
Twenty Five	141
Twenty Six	143
Twenty Seven	147
Twenty Eight	149
Twenty Nine	153
Thirty	157

Thirty One 159

Thirty Two 163

Thirty Three 167

Thirty Four 171

Thirty Five 173

Thirty Six 177

Thirty Seven 183

Thirty Eight 187

Thirty Nine 195

Fourty 199

Epilogue 205

Other Books By Samantha Baca 221

Acknowledgments 225

About the Author 227

<u>One</u>
Julie

My fingers gripped the steering wheel tightly as I struggled to maintain control of the car as it slipped on a patch of ice. Even with the heater on full blast, it was cold enough for Daisy to whimper in the back seat as she tried to sleep with a blanket wrapped around her. I hated that I had to wake her in the middle of the night without being able to tell her what was going on, but there wasn't another choice. It was either leave right then and there or stay and risk something far more dangerous happening.

It had been years since I'd been up to the inn that we used to go to when I was little, and even though I thought I knew the way to it, everything looked different. It didn't help that I was driving through a blizzard in the middle of the night and couldn't see where I was going. My hands trembled as adrenaline rushed through me, keeping me alert and focused as I tried to get us to safety.

The car was quiet so Daisy could sleep, but that did nothing to stop the images of Joel standing over me as anger flashed in his eyes from flooding my brain. I knew that our friendship had grown and changed over the years I worked for him, but I never expected things to take a turn the way they had with him.

"Do you think you can just walk away and leave me?" he yelled, standing above me as his fist shook inches away from my face. He'd already hit me once and knocked me to the floor; I knew he would do it again. "After everything that I've done for you—this is how you repay me? I gave you everything!"

I shook my head, my lips quivering as I watched the man I thought I knew transform into a monster I'd never seen before. The vein in his temple throbbed as his eyes dilated, appearing darker in the dim light.

"I wasn't leaving," I stammered, hoping he couldn't see the lie on the tip of my tongue. I also didn't want to agitate him further while Daisy was sleeping in the other room. Thankfully, her door was closed, and the sound machine was on, so hopefully it had drowned out all of this.

"I was looking at places to go on a mini vacation with Daisy. This time of year is always so hard for her. I just wanted to do something special for her."

"You need to ask for my permission first," he snarled, extending his hand as I stared at it.

His eyebrows raised as he jerked it toward me and gave me a pointed look. I carefully accepted it, trying to keep my body from shaking as I got to my feet and took a cautious step back.

"I'm sorry that I lost my temper," he said, shoving a hand through his hair. "But if this is going to work between us, there has to be communication."

"I don't understand," I whispered, immediately regretting it. "If what is going to work between us? I'm not your employee right now, and these aren't work hours. You came to my apartment uninvited and without any warning." My voice trembled as I tried to stand up for myself like I had been for the past few weeks. The only difference was that the Joel I had pushed back against and stood up to before wasn't the same Joel who was standing before me with a look in his eyes that made my blood turn to ice.

"You're not just my employee, Julie. I thought I'd made that clear? I've built a life for you and Daisy, and that includes me being part of it. There's not a single thing you can do to stop me from having what I want. I always get what I want. I'm a very determined man and you'd do well to remember that."

I nodded, too terrified to speak. It didn't matter what I said; it would be wrong unless it were me professing my love for him.

"It's getting late," he said, looking at his watch. "Can I trust that you're going to bed and that we'll talk about this more in the morning?"

"Yes. I'm very tired, so I'll be going straight to bed."

My stomach soured as I felt him lean in and press a kiss to my lips. I dug my nails into the palms of my hands, hoping the pain from it would distract me enough to keep from pulling away from him. I knew how angry he would get, and I didn't want any more trouble right now. I just needed him to leave so I could gather myself and figure out the next step.

"Sleep tight. I'll see you in the morning." He smiled, but it was empty and void of any emotion. "And Julie, don't forget that I see everything. I wouldn't try anything stupid if I were you."

I nodded again, desperate for him to leave my apartment. He turned and walked out, pulling the door closed behind him. I waited a few seconds before I rushed over and locked it, knowing it didn't really matter because he had a key and could get back in if he wanted to.

I counted to twenty as I slowly made it through the apartment, turning off lights and making it seem like I was getting ready for bed. I didn't know if he would be back and didn't want to give him anything else to be upset about.

I laid in bed for an hour, hoping that he had already fallen asleep, given how late it was. There wasn't much time to do what I needed to do, so I had to act quickly. I got up and reached under the bed, grabbing the duffel bag I had started packing a few days ago. I pulled on a pair of jeans and tennis shoes, then slung the bag over my shoulder, making sure all of the important things were in it. I rushed to Daisy's room and woke her up, hating that I had to disturb her peaceful sleep.

"Mommy? What's wrong?" she asked, her voice filled with sleep.

"We have to leave, baby. I need you to get up and put your shoes on for me, okay?"

I grabbed them and pulled a pair of socks out of her dresser before helping her.

"Where are we going?" She rubbed her eyes as she watched me.

"Someplace special and magical. But we have to hurry."

I stood up and looked at her, her hair a mess on top of her head, as her bright eyes looked up at me with confusion.

"Can I take Uni with me?"

"Of course." I smiled and grabbed her stuffed unicorn, tucking it into the duffel bag as I picked her up and made my way out of the apartment. She was too heavy to carry, but the thought of anything happening to her had me clutching her tight to my chest as she tried to wrap her legs around my waist to hold on. We got to the car, and I got her situated quickly before I jumped in and hit the gas, getting us out of there as fast as possible.

A single tear slid down my cheek as I shook my head to clear my thoughts.

This wasn't the first time I had started my life over, but I would make sure it was the last. I didn't have a plan until I thought about the last place that I truly felt safe and knew that was where I was going.

Two
Gage

I was headed to the garage to look for a tool when a dark figure showing through the frosted window of the front door startled me. I stopped and furrowed my brow as I watched the doorknob rattle as if someone were picking the lock. It was a brave thing to do, especially since we were in the middle of the woods and I didn't welcome visitors.

I flung the door open, ready to dismiss whoever was on the other side, but stopped when dark green eyes stared at me. They widened in disbelief as a reddish color tinted the cheeks that were pale from the frigid cold. A gust of wind pushed past us, sending an icy chill down my spine but I was frozen in place as I stared at her.

"Julie?" I asked, my voice sounding gruff and unwelcoming. "What are you doing here?"

"I… Um…" She pressed her lips together and then blew out a heavy breath as she stared back at me.

"Mommy, can we go inside already? My toes hurt," a little voice said, immediately pulling my attention to the small child.

My heart leapt in my chest as I saw the little girl, her features almost identical to her mother, who still stood there, staring at me.

"Come inside," I said, ignoring every question that was racing through my mind.

The little girl smiled at me and bounced inside as if she had been there a thousand times.

"Can I watch TV?" she asked, completely oblivious to her mother.

"Sure," I replied cautiously. I had no idea whether Julie wanted her to watch TV or not. But that was because I had no idea what was going on. All that I knew for sure was that my former best friend's little sister was standing in front of me with a bruise on her cheek that made my blood boil. "Get your ass inside the house, Julie."

Suddenly, it was as if something snapped her out of her thoughts as she grabbed the suitcase beside her and came inside.

I closed the door and locked it, an uneasy feeling sitting in the pit of my stomach.

"Is it okay if I put something on the TV for her?" I asked, wanting to make sure the little girl was taken care of as she curled up on my couch and petted my dog.

"You don't have to do that," she rushed out quickly, her eyes scanning the room until they settled on her daughter. "Daisy, we aren't staying so don't get too comfortable."

"But, Mom, there's a doggie," Daisy whined. "He likes me. Why aren't we staying? You said this was where we were going to spend Christmas because it was magical when you were a chi—"

"Daisy—" Julie opened her mouth to say more, but I shook my head and folded my arms over my chest as she stalled.

"Fine. She can watch TV." Her shoulders slumped in defeat.

I nodded and walked into the living room, hoping there was something kid-friendly to watch. My grandmother had a collection of DVDs that I had recently put into a donation pile, so I grabbed the box and dug through it until I found a few that seemed safe.

"The Little Mermaid or Cinderella?" I asked, holding both of them up so she could see the covers.

"The Little Mermaid!" she squealed, grabbing the blanket from the back of the couch and getting settled. "Do you have any popcorn?"

"Daisy!" Julie hissed, now standing behind her. "This isn't our house. We can't just ask for things and make ourselves at home. Besides, you haven't even had breakfast yet."

"But you said that we were going to li—" Daisy started before Julie stopped her.

"Yes. Plans have changed since then," Julie said firmly. "We will talk about it later. In private."

I watched them for a few minutes, not loving what I was hearing. Something was wrong, and I needed to know what it was.

"Do you like extra butter?" I asked Daisy, earning a hard glare from Julie as she tilted her head to the side and placed her hands firmly on her hips. At this point, it seemed irrelevant whether the child had eaten breakfast yet or not. She wanted popcorn, so she was going to get popcorn.

"Yes! Please!"

"You got it. I'll start the movie now and then bring you some popcorn in a few minutes," I said, smiling down at the adorable little girl.

I could feel the intensity of Julie's stare as she followed me into the kitchen and waited until there was enough space between us and her daughter before she began speaking.

"What the hell was that?" she demanded, pinning me with a look as she pointed at Daisy.

"The kid asked for popcorn, so I'm making some," I replied as I opened a bag and popped it in the microwave.

"You have no right to just—"

"I have no right? Are you kidding me? You showed up at my house and tried to break in."

She pressed her lips together as she shook her head.

"It's not your house," she countered.

"Really? Because I'm pretty sure the trust paperwork shows that I am the sole owner of the place now that my grandmother is dead."

"I'm sorry. I didn't know that anyone would be here. I figured since she was gone…"

"You would break in and be a modern-day Goldilocks?" I arched an eyebrow and waited for her response as the popcorn popped.

"It wasn't like that," she said with a heavy sigh as she pulled a chair out from the dining table and sat down. "I didn't know where else to go."

"I'm going to take snacks to that adorable little girl while she watches a movie, and when I come back, you and I have a lot of talking to do."

She nodded and lowered her head, watching as I took the popcorn out of the microwave and poured it into a giant bowl.

"She can't have that entire bowl," she objected, looking horrified when I grabbed a handful of individually wrapped snacks from the counter and winked at her. There was nothing I loved more than getting under her skin and had been doing it since the day I met her twenty years ago.

Three
Julie

I hadn't been prepared to see Gage, which likely explained why I had felt so flushed and antsy since we arrived. My plan had been simple: wake Daisy up in the middle of the night after I packed only what we needed, and drive the seven hours to the cabin in the woods. We would arrive by early morning and have the day to get settled in.

Only it wasn't just a cabin in the middle of the woods. It was an inn that my brother's best friend's grandmother had owned, and we would spend every summer there growing up. There were at least ten bedrooms and a large dining room that opened up into the beautiful living room that had huge windows that looked out into the forest. About half a mile away from the cabin was a lake that we would spend our days at. The boys would try their luck fishing, but would always give up after a few hours and join us as we took turns jumping off the tire swing that hung from the large maple tree.

I loved that I could still see Daisy from my spot at the dining room table, but what I didn't love was the look on Gage's face as he returned and took a seat right beside me.

"Do you need anything before we get started? Water? Food?"

"No, I'm fine. Thank you," I said softly as I leaned back in the padded chair, finally noticing how tired I felt.

"What's going on, Julie?" he asked, cutting straight to the chase.

"Nothing. I just needed somewhere to go for a few days."

"Bullshit. Don't fucking play games with me, Julie. You know I will find out, so you might as well tell me."

"It's nothing. I promise. I have it handled."

"Have what handled?"

I rolled my eyes, hating—but also secretly loving—that he thought he could force me to talk. Gage had been a lot to me over the years, but mean was never on that list. Not that he was being mean right now, but I also didn't want to cross him. I knew that he wasn't someone to mess with after the falling out he had with my brother.

"Julie," he warned, leaning back slightly in his chair, just enough that the corded muscles in his arm showed as he rested it on the table.

When had he gotten this muscular? Had his body always been like this? There was no way I would have survived my teen years with him looking like this, so it must have happened after I stopped coming around. Probably a good thing because I wanted to climb him like a tree…

He cleared his throat, forcing my attention back to him as his deep, dark brown eyes stayed focused on me.

"I don't want to talk about it," I said with a shrug. "Like I said, I didn't know anyone would be here. Now that I do, I will be out of your hair as soon as possible."

"What are you running from?"

An icy chill snaked down my back as the blood drained from my face, giving me away. While I hadn't been able to stop obsessing over everything on our way up here, I wasn't quite ready to talk about it. Doing so meant that it was real and that I couldn't just run from the nightmare and pretend it didn't happen.

"Okay—let me restate that. Who are you running from?"

I swallowed hard, looking over at Daisy as she ate her popcorn and watched the movie. I would need to figure out something healthier to feed her for lunch since it was apparent that I wasn't getting that popcorn back from her anytime soon.

"My boss." I lowered my eyes and refused to meet his gaze.

"Your boss? Did you embezzle from them or something? Am I harboring a criminal here?"

I could hear the faint hint of humor in his voice, but refused to lean into it. I didn't need anything to feel too comfortable right now, including him. As much as I wanted to joke and let things feel light again, I couldn't risk the distraction.

"No. He's been mildly obsessed with me. I didn't realize the gravity of it until I found him in my apartment the other day when I got home."

His eyebrows rose quickly as he leaned forward and stared at me.

"Are you fucking kidding me?"

"I wish I were," I said with a nervous laugh.

"Start talking. I want to know everything."

"Gage, we don't need to do all of this. It's fine. I just need a few hours to reset, and then we will be on our way."

"Like fucking hell you will," he growled. "If you honestly think you can show up here and tell me that some asshole is obsessed with you and think that I'm going to allow you to leave, you are seriously mistaken, Julie."

"You can't force me to stay here."

"No. You're right," he said, shaking his head as his jaw clenched tightly. "But that storm outside can. Or did you not notice it on your way in?"

I looked out the window he pointed to, watching as the snow fell heavily in sheets. Not only had I noticed it on the way in, but I had lost traction on the road several times and thought I was going to crash by the time I pulled up to the cabin. I had been so thankful to get here that I must not have noticed his vehicle parked outside. Had I seen it, I might have made a different decision than to try to break in and hide out here.

"There's no way you're going anywhere in that storm, Julie. Not until it passes and the roads are safe to drive again."

"We can't stay here and impose on you," I objected, throwing my hands in the air.

"You were planning to stay here before you found out I was here," he countered. "So don't play games with me, Julie.

You made the arrangements you needed because you knew you would be here for a while, didn't you?"

A faint blush crept up my cheeks as I tried to look away.

He was right. I had been packing the car with food and necessities for weeks once I started to notice the change with Joel. Deep down, I knew I would end up leaving but I couldn't risk tipping him off before I was ready to flee. Every time I went grocery shopping, I would buy more than we needed and hide some items in the back of the car under blankets so no one could see what they were. I had packed enough food to last us a month or two and prayed that we would be lucky enough to have access to running water and electricity once we arrived. I had no idea if things had been shut off after Gage's grandmother died, but I didn't have any other option than to run to the only place that had ever felt safe.

"Where is the rest of your stuff?" he asked, folding his hands in front of him as he watched me. "The stuff you planned to use while you stayed here?"

"In the trunk of my car," I replied softly, staring down at the floor.

"Give me your keys. I'll go grab everything before the storm gets worse."

"You don't have to—"

"Julie—the keys. Give them to me."

I reached into my pocket and pulled them out, sliding them across the table and ignoring the jolt of electricity that ran through me as his fingers brushed mine.

Staying with Gage brought a sense of security that I hadn't realized I needed. It also brought a sense of dread because there was no way I was going to be able to constantly be around him and hide the feelings I had been harboring for years.

Four
Gage

My mind had been racing since the moment Julie said she was running from her boss and I hadn't been able to stop obsessing over needing all of the information she refused to give me. When I saw how much stuff she had packed with her, I knew that she wasn't just running from someone, but that she didn't have any plans of going back.

Part of me hoped that it was just because her daughter was there and she didn't want to worry her, but another part of me worried that she wouldn't open up to me because of the current status of my friendship with her brother.

"Does she like macaroni and cheese?" I asked Julie as I stared in the fridge for kid-friendly dinner options.

"She's not a picky eater, and like I said, you don't have to cook for us."

I closed the door and turned around to stare at her.

"If you truly think that I will cook for myself and not make enough for every person in this house, then you don't know me at all."

Lunch had been a battle as well, with Julie fighting me over making a ton of grilled cheese sandwiches and insisting she didn't need me to take care of them. It wasn't that I felt like I needed to take care of them, but more so that I wanted to.

"I didn't mean it like that," she replied, sighing heavily. "I just feel bad that you're doing all of this cooking for us. That's extra work that you didn't ask for."

"It's literally not any extra work. I just need to know what she likes. I don't want to make something and she only eats it because she feels like she has to. I want her to like it."

"Well, she's probably still full from the popcorn and snacks you loaded her up with earlier," Julie teased, walking beside me in the kitchen as she dug through one of the paper bags filled with food I had brought in from her car earlier. I had insisted on storing everything in the pantry for her, but she was still reluctant to do anything that might insinuate they would be staying with me for a while. Even when I showed them around the house and let them pick which bedrooms they wanted, I could see the anxiety rolling off of Julie as her mind raced with trying to figure out another option.

"She ate her lunch just fine," I objected with raised hands. But she was right, I had given in and let Daisy have more snacks after lunch because I couldn't say no to her adorable little face.

"Since you're being so nice about it and won't take no for an answer, this is her favorite macaroni and cheese."

She handed me a box that had cartoon dogs on it and smirked.

"You want me to make her dog macaroni?" I questioned,

holding the box and examining it as I turned it around and looked at the other side.

"It doesn't have actual dogs in it." She laughed. "But this is her favorite cartoon to watch, so she will be excited when she sees it."

"Wait—she hasn't had this one before?" I asked, hating how excited I was to impress a child.

"No." She shook her head. "I grabbed it at the store the other day, but didn't have a chance to show her yet. After everything happened, my mind was kind of scattered. But it will be a nice surprise for her here."

I nodded as if I weren't affected by this at all. I didn't want to come across as overly invested in things and scare her off, even though deep down I hated that something bad had happened, which left Julie and her daughter in danger.

While she worked on fixing a salad with the vegetables I had in the fridge, I focused on following the directions on the back of the box because I wasn't going to be the one who ruined Daisy's favorite macaroni.

****

After dinner, I finished preparing the guest room for Julie while she gave Daisy a bath. While I had come up to the cabin with the intention of clearing it out so I could sell it, I hadn't been there long before Julie showed up this morning. I had arrived the day before and had only enough time to unpack the essentials, knowing I would be there for a few weeks, thanks to the storm rolling in. Being a general contractor meant I didn't have to hire anyone to come out and do the work that needed to be done.

Before dinner, I threw some linens in the wash so they would have fresh towels in the guest bathroom, and clean sheets and blankets for their bed. I had offered them any room in the house, aside from the one I had already taken. But instead of taking one with two beds, Julie chose the one right next to mine, which had a king-sized bed. She insisted that it made her feel better to have Daisy close to her, but I couldn't stop myself from hoping that they would both feel safer being in the room right next to me.

I sat on the couch, pretending to watch TV while Duke laid beside me, tired from a long afternoon of cuddling with Daisy. I didn't know if Julie would come out and talk with me once she got Daisy to sleep, but I hoped she would. I needed to talk to her and get answers to the questions that wouldn't stop infiltrating my thoughts.

The news began with the meteorologist discussing how this storm would be greater than anything they'd seen before. I'd lived in Washington, close to Mount Rainier, for most of my life, so I knew how bad the snow could get. This storm seemed to be having a "hold my beer" moment with what the expected snowfall was forecasted to be. All of us were guaranteed to be snowed in for at least a few days—if not more. Thankfully, between what I brought with me and what Julie had, we had plenty of food to get us through until the roads were clear again and we could get to the store.

"Thank you again for letting us stay. She's out like a light," Julie said as she sat down beside me on the couch and curled her legs underneath her.

"It's not a problem at all." I grabbed the remote and turned the TV off so I could have her full attention. I didn't want to force it out of her, but I needed to know what happened. I needed to be able to protect them, and I could only do that if I knew what they were up against.

"I know you don't want to, but I need you to tell me what happened," I said softly, hoping it would encourage her to talk to me. I knew that my rough exterior tended to keep people away—the way I liked it. But I didn't want that with Julie. If anything, I wanted her closer so she could feel the strength of my protection and know that I would do anything in the world to keep her and Daisy safe. I wanted her to hear my heart as it beat steadily in my chest, beating for them, because reconnecting with Julie sent shockwaves through my body, reminding me of the feelings I had kept hidden from her for all these years.

"I don't even know where to start." She pressed her lips together and let her shoulders drop as she exhaled heavily. "When I first met Joel, my boss, it was when I was in between jobs right after Mike died. Daisy had just turned one, and I was lost trying to figure out how to be a single mom while grieving the death of my husband and trying to pay our bills. Joel offered me a position where I could work from home so I didn't have to worry about finding childcare."

I shifted slightly on the couch to see her better, but stayed quiet so she could continue.

"I didn't have family close by to help out with my parents living in Florida and Patrick moving to New York for his new job. He offered to come help us, but I couldn't do that to him. I knew how hard he'd worked for that promotion, and after Melanie called off their engagement, I knew he needed a fresh start. He didn't need to be tied down with taking care of his little sister and her child."

"I know that Patrick and I have our differences, but I can assure you that your brother would have dropped everything to help you, Julie. He loves you more than anything. He was so thrilled to be an uncle. Nothing could ever keep him from you guys."

"I know," she said with a soft smile. "But I just couldn't do that to him. I think part of me wanted to prove to myself that I could do this on my own. And for a while, I did. Things were going great and I was able to work from home while taking care of Daisy. Then everything started to change this year when she started kindergarten. It was hard having her away from me all the time, but I loved how happy she was about going to school. She would come home and talk my ear off from the moment I picked her up, telling me every single thing that happened that day."

She laughed softly as the memories replayed in her mind, and I grinned because I could absolutely see that happening. I had only spent one day with Daisy, and she had been the most lively, most animated child I had ever met. The passion that sparkled in her eyes when she told me about her hobbies and how much she loved school was so intense that I couldn't imagine going through the rest of my life and not hearing about hers.

"But then once she was in school, I started to notice that Joel was acting differently. We'd had the same schedule for almost four years, and suddenly, things didn't work for him anymore." She tipped her head back and rolled it slowly on her shoulders before looking at me. "At first, I thought it was because I was able to work more hours, so it made sense that he needed me more. But then, a few months ago, he started just showing up at my apartment for meetings. It was really weird because we never did in-person meetings, and when I asked him about it, he said that it was mandatory for all employees. I offered to go into the office for the meetings now that Daisy was in school, but he insisted that we do it in my office, which of course was in my living room."

My jaw tightened as I listened, already knowing that I would hate where this was going.

"It was little things here and there, most of which I tried to ignore. When I asked him to mark all our meetings on the shared calendar in advance, he got angry and said that I didn't get to choose how he ran his company. While it seemed weird, I didn't question it because I didn't want to lose my job. I was able to take care of Daisy and make ends meet, so I didn't want to press my luck. But last month, I went out and did my grocery shopping during my lunch hour, and when I got back, he was in my apartment waiting for me."

"Are you fucking kidding me?"

"No. I wish I were."

"How did he get into your apartment?"

"He told the superintendent that I said it was okay for him to have a key. When I questioned why they would just give it to him, he told me that he explained that I was using the apartment as office space and that I was his employee. He showed the superintendent the paperwork confirming my employment and that the office address listed on my employee record matched the address of the apartment."

"Julie, that's fucking illegal," I growled, ready to go find this asshole.

"I know. Trust me, I was already trying to figure out how to get out of the situation before it got worse. I couldn't just quit my job and leave because I didn't have any money in savings, and we had nowhere to go. But then he started making it a point to show up unexpectedly during the week when Daisy was in school and made excuses about why he needed to see me. He never gave me any advance notice, and when he came in two weeks ago while I was in the shower, that was my final straw."

"Fucking hell, Julie," I said as I sighed heavily and shoved a hand through my hair.

"It's been a mess, and I've been doing everything I can to try to get us out of it. I've been buying extra non-perishable groceries and storing them in the car so he wouldn't notice anything out of the ordinary. I had to leave most of our stuff behind because I couldn't let him on to us leaving. I knew he wouldn't allow me to. He had made it apparent that he thought I was his property because I was his employee. As long as I lived in that apartment, he felt he could come and go whenever he wanted to."

"You should have called the police or—"

"And what? Tell them that my boss was being inappropriate? I did, Gage. I talked to someone about him stalking me and knowing where I was when I wasn't at home. I told them about the creepy notes he started leaving me on work documents when he would come by to drop them off. I told them about the unwanted touches that he refused to stop doing. And do you want to know what they said?"

"Probably not," I admitted, already knowing it would piss me off.

"They said that I could file a complaint with the HR department at work. Our non-existent HR department."

"Wow."

"Yeah, wow. Trust me, I have been beating myself up over my stupidity for so long that there's nothing you can say that will make me feel worse about this than I already do. What kind of person goes to work for someone who doesn't even have an HR department? I mean, I should have seen the red flags sooner. I worked for him for four years, Gage. Four years. I never noticed anything was wrong until Daisy started school."

"He was probably just waiting for her to start so he could start moving in and going after what he wanted," I said angrily.

"Yeah, he made that glaringly obvious when he tried to kiss me the other day. I pushed him off, and he got angry. I saw a side of him that I hadn't ever seen before. He'd always been so nice and soft-spoken. But something changed, and he snapped. He pinned me against the wall and rubbed himself against me, telling me how he could tell that I wanted him. He insisted that I was playing hard to get. When I told him that I wasn't interested and that he was making me uncomfortable, he hit me. He held me by my throat until I couldn't breathe. I tried everything, Gage. It wasn't until I started crying that he backed off. He was so pissed that he threw my vase across the room and left the broken glass on the floor as he stormed out and told me he would be back to finish what we started."

"Did you ever consider changing the locks?"

I didn't want to make her feel worse than she already did,

but I also couldn't wrap my head around all of this without wanting to murder the bastard.

"I had them changed twice before he informed me that if I changed them again, he would fire me for destruction of company property."

"But that's not company property—that's your fucking apartment."

"Yeah, I thought so, too. And then he showed me that he had taken over the monthly rent on my apartment, starting that month. He claimed that because I worked from home, that space was my office and the company was required to pay for it, just as they would for office space for any other employees."

"Do other employees work from home, too? Does he pay their rent?"

"I don't know. I've never been to the office, so I'm not sure if there are any other employees. It turns out I don't know a lot about the man I've been supposedly working for the past four years. All of our video meetings were always just the two of us. I do data entry for him, so it's not like I've had any reason to meet with anyone else. My job was always simple and he said it was to help him stay organized and on track." She let out a nervous laugh. "I wouldn't be surprised if the company doesn't even exist and I've just been being played this entire time."

"Julie, that's fucking scary," I said in disbelief. I scrubbed a hand down my face and let out a shaky, frustrated breath. "Where did you meet him? Didn't you go in for an interview or something before you got the job?"

She shook her head as a few tears slid down her face.

"I met him right after Mike's funeral. It was a few days after the service, and I was sitting at a café looking at job listings while Daisy slept in her stroller. I had dark sunglasses on to try to hide my grief, but I was so consumed by it. I didn't know where to go or what to do. I didn't want to end up a homeless, widowed, single mother wandering the streets with a baby she couldn't afford to keep. I was desperate, and he must have sensed it. He sat at the table across from me, and when I started crying, he came over and offered me a tissue. He seemed so nice that I didn't think twice before I told him my life story. I expected him to walk away, but instead, he offered me a job and it felt like the grief lifted slightly. There was hope when I thought I would never feel it again. I was so relieved to have a job that I accepted without asking any questions." She tipped her head forward as more tears spilled down her face, as she covered it with her hands. "I was so stupid. So fucking stupid, Gage. After last night, I knew I had to leave."

"What happened last night?"

"He came into my apartment uninvited, asking for a report I had been working on. When I went to get it, he made himself at home at my computer and was looking at my recent search history. He was pissed that I was looking at rental cabins in the middle of nowhere and attacked me. He hit me, and I fell to the ground as he stood over me, yelling about how I could never leave. I lied and said I was looking up places to take Daisy on vacation. I don't know if he bought it or not, but it got him to stop. He left, but he said that I should remember he sees everything. I waited an hour or so after he left, then I grabbed what I could and we left. I drove straight here, not even giving it any thought that someone might be here." She stopped for a second as tears welled in her eyes. "I just always felt safe here, and I wanted to feel that again."

She closed her eyes and let herself cry as I scooted across the couch, closing the small gap between us, and pulled her into my arms. I held her as she fell apart, letting all of the weight of her emotions go as she wept against my chest.

I wanted to promise her that everything would be okay and that I would take care of them, but I didn't want to do something stupid, like fall in love with my former best friend's little sister.

Loving Julie was easy. It always had been.

But trying to keep myself from falling for her right now would be the hardest thing I've ever had to do.

Five
Julie

I had slept so good after falling asleep in Gage's arms that I hadn't even noticed that he had tucked me into bed beside Daisy until I woke up to her arms wrapped around my stomach as she snored soundly beside me. I rubbed my eyes and looked around, feeling comforted that we were in the same room I had spent so many years of my childhood in.

The sun peeked through the sheer curtains, letting me know that it was time to get up. I didn't want to wake her, so I gently pulled her arm off of me and slipped out of bed, thankful that it didn't creak. The house was old, but it had been well-maintained over the years.

I grabbed my phone from the nightstand and crept out of the bedroom, pulling the door behind me. I didn't want it all the way closed so I could hear her, but I also didn't want anything to wake her up until she was ready to start her day. It had been a long day yesterday, with her being restless on our way up here and not sleeping in the car like I had wanted her to.

When I walked into the kitchen, I stopped dead in my tracks. I tried to swallow, but my throat was suddenly dry as my heart hammered in my chest.

Standing at the kitchen island was Gage, sipping a cup of coffee as he looked at something on his phone. The problem wasn't that he was absolutely the most gorgeous-looking man I had seen in a while—it was that he was standing there wearing nothing but a pair of low-hanging sweats that highlighted the deep V that my eyes were drawn to.

"Good morning," he said, lifting his eyes for a split second to acknowledge me before returning his attention to his phone.

I folded my arms in front of my chest, attempting to hide my nipples that decided to say hello for me. I rolled my eyes and shook my head as I muttered something about how it would be a good morning if I weren't being tortured by his fucking body as I walked past him.

"What was that?" he asked, looking over his shoulder as I rounded the corner of the island and stared at the coffee maker to keep from looking at him.

"I said, good morning," I lied, forcing a smile as I glanced at him quickly before returning my focus to figuring out the fancy machine.

I wasn't the kind of girl who spent a lot of money—or energy—on coffee, which meant that I had no idea how to make this stupid thing work. I just needed a plain, simple cup of coffee that could be poured from an old school carafe. My brows furrowed together as I stared at the buttons and tried to make sense of them.

"Need help?" he offered, his voice irritatingly soothing and slightly silky this morning.

I pressed my thighs together and scolded my vagina for

trying to act like a damn fool. He's asking about coffee—not if you'd like a good pounding. Which I would…

"Umm," I cleared my throat as I began pressing random buttons. "No. I think I've got it. Thanks."

He set his cup and phone down as he walked over and stood behind me. The heat of his body radiated off him and sent chills along my skin. I held my breath to keep from inhaling his scent, which was a combination of pine and citrus—something that made the urge to turn around and nuzzle my face in his splatting of chest hair almost too much to control.

"You have to select a cup size first," he said as he reached forward, his arm brushing against my shoulder and sending another wave of chills across my skin.

I looked up at the ceiling and tried to ignore every instinct because my body was about to betray me any second now.

"How much do you want?"

My eyes widened as I watched his finger, so long and slender as it hovered over the buttons. I could imagine that finger teasing my body and bringing me immense pleasure as it rubbed my clit until I spasmed around it.

"Julie," he said with a hint of humor in his tone while his other hand landed gently on my waist. "You okay?"

"Yeah," I replied shakily. My body was on fire with need for this man, and he had barely even touched me. Not only that—it wasn't even a sexual touch. It just showed how long it had been since I had any real affection or human touch and how badly my body craved it.

"How big do you want it?"

Shit. How big could he get it? I wasn't trying to be a creep, but it wasn't like his gray sweatpants were doing anything to hide the morning wood he was sporting when I walked in. He had to be a good eight to nine inches—if not more. And that was just length. I couldn't tell for sure since I had just stolen a glance, but I was pretty confident that I saw a good amount of girth there, too.

"For your coffee, Julie," he continued, giving my side a tender squeeze to get my attention. But if anything, it just made it worse. His hand was on my body, showing me how firm he could be with his touch, which only made me imagine him grabbing my ass or fondling my breasts. His body was so close to mine that I could feel the faint outline of said erection.

"I don't think I need coffee this morning," I muttered, too frustrated to try to figure this out. What I needed was a solid fifteen minutes by myself with my trusted rose. That always did the trick.

"Oh? What is that you need instead?" he asked, his words deliberate as he spun me around and pressed my back against the island, pinning me to it.

His dark eyes searched mine as he subtly licked his lips. I sucked in a sharp breath as I tried to calm the storm raging inside as my body begged him for relief.

"I don't know," I whispered breathlessly, trying to look away.

But then his hand slid up until his fingers pinched the bottom of my chin and forced me to look at him.

"You know there's nothing in this world I won't give you, Julie," he said as he licked his lips again. "All you have to do is say the word and I'll make it happen."

Fuck. Me.

No, seriously—fuck me. Right here. Right now. Forget the coffee and the storm raging outside, and just fuck me like I need to be fucked.

"It sounds like Daisy is up," he said, cocking his head to the side as he heard something. He completely interrupted my thoughts as he stepped away and looked over his shoulder. "I'm going to go shower and clean up. Let me know what you girls would like for breakfast, and I'll make it when I come back."

The air whooshed out of me in a frustrated breath as I watched him turn around and leave.

Staying with Gage might be even more dangerous than being on the run from Joel.

<u>Six</u>
Gage

I had been a fucking idiot.

I knew better than to allow myself to slip around Julie, but I couldn't help myself.

Last night, when she let me hold her while she cried and then fell asleep in my arms, it changed something. Something inside of me snapped, and I was no longer just her brother's (ex) best friend. I was a man on a mission to protect what was mine, and I felt a ferocity that ran through my blood, knowing I would do anything to keep her and Daisy safe.

The problem was that she wasn't mine to protect. She was the one woman I wasn't supposed to fall for—ever. Patrick had made that abundantly clear during our teen years when my attraction to Julie reached an all-time high. But pushing him aside, I knew that it wasn't right to fall for her right now. She didn't need someone stepping in and trying to seduce her—she needed someone who would keep her safe. Someone who would lay their life on the line to make sure no harm ever came to either of them.

Instead, I decided to let my dick talk this morning, and he was quite the chatty bastard.

There was no doubt that Julie had felt my erection this morning, given how close I had gotten to her. But trying to stop it was like trying to tell a man not to drink the water when stranded in the desert—it was stupid and didn't make sense. Then again, when it came to Julie, nothing made sense at the moment.

I pulled out the stuff I needed for the pancakes I was making for Daisy and tried to focus on cooking instead of thinking about Julie and how good she smelled as she walked through the kitchen with her hair wet from the shower.

"Did you convince Gage to make you pancakes?" she asked Daisy, ruffling her hair as she passed by, smiling at her daughter as she handed her a unicorn stuffed animal.

"He offered," Daisy replied with a shrug as she squeezed the toy and smiled.

"That is true," I said with a wink as I added way too many chocolate chips, ignoring the ping from my phone sitting on the counter beside me.

"You're going to have to learn to say no," Julie teased, raising her eyebrows and giving me a look that was meant to be scolding but was adorable and playful instead.

"I thought I made myself clear this morning that when it comes to you and Daisy, I will never say no." I swallowed hard, allowing myself to taste the truth in the words I had spoken.

Julie's cheeks flushed the slightest shade of pink as she blushed and looked away.

"I would have made breakfast," she said, changing the subject. "You don't have to keep cooking for us."

"Like I said, I don't mind. I would be making food for myself regardless. Making extra isn't as big of a deal as you seem to think it is."

"So you typically make yourself chocolate chip pancakes and twenty slices of bacon for breakfast?" She put her hand on her hip and tilted her head as she studied me with a knowing grin.

"As a matter of fact, I do. I like to enjoy the weekend and sometimes indulge in a fun breakfast, thank you very much." I made sure to use my most playful tone as I shook my head at Julie, earning a giggle from Daisy.

Fuck, I loved the way that little girl laughed. Almost as much as I loved the smile on her face. She was such a happy child, and it was contagious because there was no way anyone could be unhappy around Daisy.

"You're so full of shit," Julie whispered, but loud enough that Daisy heard her.

"That's a bad word, Mommy," Daisy said, moving the unicorn on the island as if it were walking around.

Just then, my phone dinged again on the counter beside me. I looked down and frowned, my blood running ice cold when I saw the alert: AirTag Detected.

My head whipped around as I stared at the toy in Daisy's arms, the panic etched deeply on my face.

"What's wrong?" Julie asked, looking from me to her daughter, who was still oblivious to the fact that anything was wrong.

"Nothing," I lied. "Breakfast is ready. Why don't you take Daisy to the couch and put on a movie while I make her a plate?"

Julie nodded with her brow still furrowed. I didn't want to scare Daisy and freak out before I could confirm what was happening, so I couldn't just come out and say it.

"Make sure she leaves the stuffed animal on the island," I whispered in her ear as I leaned around to grab a plate.

She let out a soft gasp as her eyes darted to the toy.

"Why don't we go put on a movie?" she asked Daisy, turning the chair to the side and helping her down as she set the toy on the island out of her reach.

"I want to take Uni," Daisy objected, reaching for the toy.

"We don't want to risk getting her dirty. You can have her after breakfast, okay?"

Daisy shrugged and followed Julie into the living room, climbing up onto her favorite spot on the couch as I finished putting her breakfast together. Julie grabbed the remote and put a movie on for Daisy while I put her plate on the tray she had been using, while Duke laid protectively beside her.

"I'll bring you some juice," Julie said, not noticing that Daisy wasn't even paying attention anymore as the cartoon dalmations ran across the screen.

"Are you going to tell me what's going on?" she asked quietly as we headed the short distance back to the island where the toy was sitting.

"My phone got an alert that there was an AirTag Detected,"

I said softly, keeping my voice low. "It didn't start notifying me until Daisy started moving the unicorn."

Julie's eyebrows rose high on her forehead as she stared at me in disbelief.

"Are you kidding me? You're saying that there is a tracking device in my daughter's toy?"

"It appears so. Possibly not the toy, but somewhere in the house."

"Can you locate it?"

"Yeah," I said with a heavy sigh. "It should let me pull it up in the Find My app, and then we can see where exactly it is."

Julie nodded as she chewed her lower lip and folded her arms over her chest protectively. We both glanced at Daisy, making sure she was okay before I pulled out my phone and clicked on the notification. The Find My app opened, and I pressed the button for it to continue until I was offered the option to play a sound. I looked up at Julie, took a deep breath, and then pressed it.

Several short, high-pitched chiming noises came from inside the unicorn, leaving both Julie and me stunned as we stared at it in disbelief.

I set my phone down and picked up the unicorn, examining it to see where the AirTag might have been inserted. Along the bottom of the toy, there was a Velcro closure. I pulled it open, noticing the battery box inside the stuffed animal. My brows furrowed in confusion until Julie spoke.

"It lights up," she explained, nodding to the battery pack.

"I turned it off the other night when we left so it wouldn't light up in the car while she was supposed to be sleeping."

I nodded and pushed it to the side, and then moved my fingers around, trying to locate the AirTag. It was a tight fit, so there wasn't much room for something to stay hidden, but we both knew it was in there somewhere. I pulled on the battery pack, trying to see if something could be hidden beneath it, but it was stuck in there.

Just as I was about to give up, I ran my finger along the top by the Velcro and stopped when I felt it. I grinned with satisfaction as I pulled the AirTag out and held it in the air.

"That fucking—" Julie started and then stopped when Daisy turned and asked for some juice.

She shook her head and then hurried off to get Daisy her drink while I went through the prompts on my phone to disable it before opening it and removing the battery. When she came back, her skin was pale, and I could see how little she had been sleeping lately. I hadn't noticed the exhaustion yesterday, but today it was more evident with the worry marring her features.

"How long do you think it's been in there?" she asked, nodding to the AirTag as she pulled out a chair and sat beside me.

"It's hard to say. My phone picked it up as soon as you brought the unicorn in here, but I ignored the first alert."

"I wonder why my phone didn't get any alerts?"

I shrugged, not sure how to answer that.

"Do you have your settings turned on?"

"Yeah. I made sure they were turned on after Mike's accident," she said softly, lowering her head as the memory washed over her. "I promised my parents that I would make sure they could always find me, just in case they needed to."

"Have you checked your settings lately?" I asked, trying to ignore the feeling in my gut.

She shook her head and pulled her phone out of her pocket before quickly swiping through different screens. She pressed her lips together and exhaled heavily through her nose.

"My location services are turned off, and the Find My feature is off as well."

"Maybe there was a system update that—"

"Stop. We both know what really happened, so there's no use in trying to make light of it. That asshole disabled them on my phone so I wouldn't know that he put a tracking device in the stuffed animal he gave my daughter."

The anger in her voice only fueled the fire that was already coursing through my veins.

"Wait—what? He gave that to Daisy?"

She nodded and pushed another heavy breath out through her pursed lips. I knew she was struggling to keep it together so she didn't upset Daisy, but this was too much.

"It was her first day of kindergarten gift he gave to her," she said with a grim smile. "Right before he started letting himself into my apartment, even when I wasn't there."

I inhaled deeply and leaned back against the chair as I stared at the AirTag, realizing this was a whole lot worse than it seemed when she first showed up here yesterday. If he had been tracking her this entire time, then that meant he knew exactly where she was.

<u>Seven</u>
Julie

The first few days of staying with Gage were actually better than I had anticipated. I knew that it might be odd, given his issues with my brother, but I couldn't have predicted how kind and caring he would be toward me and Daisy. Though, in all fairness, I should have known better because throughout all the years I'd known him, Gage had never been anything but kind.

I had been antsy ever since he found the AirTag in Daisy's stuffed unicorn, but I was relieved when we hadn't found any more. We did some research and found that if Joel tried to track it, Gage's place would be the last location that it showed. Eventually, he would come looking for us, but for now, I was relying on the raging blizzard outside to keep him away. At least it gave me a few days to figure out my next steps.

I had just finished my shower and was heading to the living room to check on Daisy when my phone rang. I pulled it out of my pocket and checked the caller ID, smiling when I saw my brother's name on the screen.

"Hey, Pat," I said happily, stopping immediately when I heard his tone.

"What the fuck is going on, Julie?"

There was so much panic in his voice that I froze, my heart dropping to my stomach.

"What do you mean?"

"I just got a call from your boss that he hasn't seen you in four days and that he's worried about you. He said that you had an emotional breakdown and then suddenly just vanished. He said that he's worried about Daisy, that you hinted you might do some—"

"I would never hurt her," I hissed, pressing the phone tighter against my ear. "He's lying, and everything is okay."

"Where are you?"

"I can't really say right now," I said, chewing my nail nervously as Gage's eyes landed on me and his eyebrows furrowed.

"Can I watch Beauty and the Beast again?" Daisy asked Gage. "Belle is my favorite princess."

"Is that Daisy?" Patrick asked, hearing more than I thought he'd be able to.

"Yes."

"Okay," he replied with a heavy sigh. "What the hell is going on, Julie? Are you okay? None of this sounds like something you'd—" He stopped mid-sentence as Gage asked Daisy if she wanted popcorn.

"Where the fuck are you?" my brother growled, his irritation and anger now overriding the panic I heard a few minutes ago.

"It's a long story that I don't really have the time to get into right now," I said softly, wincing as I heard my brother mutter a curse word on the other line.

"Tell me you are not at Gage's house," he bit out.

"Not technically."

"Julie…" he warned.

"I went to his grandmother's inn. I didn't know he'd be here," I explained as Gage walked over and stood in front of me.

"I swear to God, if that mother fucker even—"

"Even what?" Gage asked, folding his arms over his chest.

I frowned and tilted my head before pulling my phone away, wondering if I somehow accidentally put it on speaker phone.

Nope, my brother was just that loud.

Giving up on trying to keep the conversation civil, I pressed the button to put the call on speakerphone and held it in front of me. Thankfully, Daisy was already invested in her movie, so she didn't seem to care about what we were discussing.

"You better stay the fuck away from my sister," Patrick warned.

"Or what?" Gage retorted.

"Enough," I scolded, giving Gage a pointed look. "We don't have time for this."

They both stayed silent for more than a few seconds, so I continued.

"Pat, if my boss calls you again, I need you to promise that you won't give him any information about me or where I'm at. Okay?"

"No, Julie, not okay. I have no idea what's going on, so until I'm in the loop, I'm not promising shit."

"It's a lot to explain, and I can't really talk freely right now, but please trust that I did what I had to do in order to keep me and Daisy safe. I don't work for Joel anymore, and I won't be returning to my apartment."

"Is he…"

"I don't know what you're hinting at, but let's just say the answer is yes. Whatever the worst thing is that you're conjuring up in your mind—the answer is yes. Please do not send anything to the apartment, as he has access to it. For now, I will be here with Gage until the storm passes. After that, I will be looking at trading my car in for something different and changing my phone number. I may be off grid for a while, so I need you to understand that and maybe fill mom and dad in as needed."

"I'm supposed to hear all of this and trust that you're okay? Do you hear what you just said?"

"Yes. I am well aware of how bad things are right now, Patrick, and I am doing the best that I can."

"I'm going to look at flights out and see how quickly I can get there," Pat said.

"You don't need to do that."

"You're my sister, Julie. There's nothing in this world that will ever stand in my way of protecting you and Daisy."

"I know, and I love you for that. But I need you to stay where you are for right now. You couldn't get out here anyway. This blizzard is no joke, and the roads won't be cleared for days. Just stay where you are, and I'll keep you updated. Okay?"

"Fine. But I need you to do me a favor," he said as Gage shifted beside me.

"That depends on what it is," I replied flatly.

"Give the phone to Gage and take it off speakerphone. I need to speak privately with him."

The color drained from my face as I let out a small whoosh of air.

"Pat, I don't really think—"

"It's fine," Gage said reassuringly as he held his hand out for the phone. "I'll be good. I promise."

"I don't know that you're the one I'm worried about."

I shook my head and handed Gage the phone.

"I love you, Pat. Be nice."

"I love you too, Jules. Tell my niece that I love her and I'll see her soon for Christmas."

I opened my mouth to question him about that, but Gage shook his head, so I let it go. I watched as he pressed the button to take the call off speakerphone and head to his bedroom so I couldn't eavesdrop even if I wanted to.

I took a deep breath and released it slowly as I went into the living room and plopped down on the couch beside Daisy, where I could get lost in a fictional world for a little while.

Eight
Gage

I knew that Julie was going to be pissed once she heard what her brother wanted to talk to me about, which was exactly why I didn't tell her. It wasn't that I wanted to be a dick about it, but he was right—the best way to protect Julie and Daisy was to make sure we eliminated the threat directly.

Growing up with Patrick quickly taught me how short-tempered he was and how long he could hold a grudge. Just because we spoke for the first time in four years didn't mean that it was progress of any sort in mending our friendship. Things were still as rocky between us as they had been the day he looked me dead in the eye and said he never wanted to speak to me again.

I didn't worry about Patrick handling things for his little sister. The one I worried about was Joel, because when Patrick was pissed off, he would set the whole fucking world on fire.

And me? Well, I was more than happy to hand him the matches if it meant keeping Julie and Daisy safe.

Nine
Julie

I hated that Gage wouldn't tell me what Patrick wanted to talk to him about. It had been eating at me all afternoon, and every time I would try to approach it, he would shake his head at me and walk away. I didn't even have to say anything—it was like he just knew what I was going to say.

We were in the middle of making dinner while Daisy colored at the coffee table in the living room when my phone rang. I cleaned my hands on the dishtowel and pulled it out of my pocket, feeling relieved when I saw Patrick's name. Perhaps he was calling to update me on their conversation.

"Hey," I said as I answered and pressed the phone between my ear and shoulder so I could finish cutting the veggies for the fajitas. "What's up?"

"I wanted to talk to you about Christmas."

"Okay. What about it?"

"Well, since it's only two weeks away, I talked with Mom and Dad. We all thought it would be nice to spend the holiday together this year."

I frowned as I set the knife down on the cutting board and processed what he said.

"You're kidding me, right?"

"No, Jules. I'm not kidding. I think it would be great for all of us to spend Christmas together. We haven't done that since—"

"I'm aware of the last time we were all together for Christmas," I interrupted, not wanting to hear him say it.

My heart hammered in my chest as I remembered the last Christmas we had all spent together as a family. It was the one we celebrated before Mike was killed in a car accident a few weeks later, and my life was forever shattered, along with my heart.

"All I'm saying is that it would be nice to have family there to support you and Daisy," he said, his tone softer.

"We're okay," I lied, even though we were for the moment. But what happened after we left the safety of Gage's grandmother's inn was something I didn't want to think about just yet. I knew I would have to eventually, but for now, I wanted to live in the false sense of security I had been clinging to since the morning we arrived and Gage answered the door.

"Julie, you can't be so stubborn all the time," Patrick said with a heavy sigh. "This guy, Joel, isn't who you think he is. He's dangerous, and I'm genuinely worried about you."

"Yeah, I know."

"But do you? Do you really know who he is? Because what I've found so far is terrifying, Julie. The thought of him getting close to you or Daisy again makes my blood boil."

I was about to agree with him when something stopped me.

"Wait—what do you mean the stuff you've found?" I asked, my eyes cutting to Gage, who purposely turned away from me so I couldn't see his face.

"I did some digging."

"Patrick!" I scolded, forcing a smile when Daisy turned and looked to see what was happening. "I can handle this. I promise. You don't need to get involved in this. It's better for everyone if you don't."

"It's a little too late for that," he replied. "Shit, I have to take this call real quick. Can I call you back in a few minutes?"

"Yeah. That's fine."

Before I could say anything more, the line was dead. I set my phone down and turned toward Gage, allowing my heated stare to burn into the back of his head.

"I'm not going to tell you anything, so you can stop with the death stare," he said from over his shoulder as he continued cutting the meat for dinner.

I sucked in a long, deep breath and let it out slowly. Before I could badger him about what he wasn't telling me, my phone rang again. I picked it up without looking at the screen and answered it.

"You have a lot of explaining to do," I said, resting my hand on my hip. While he was my older brother, I wasn't going to just let him get away with intruding on things in my life that weren't his to worry about.

"Well, I could say the same to you."

I gasped as my hand flew to my mouth and covered it. My eyes widened with fear as Gage spun around and rushed to my side.

"Like why you felt it was necessary to leave in the middle of the night," Joel said, his tone filled with anger. "I thought we talked about that and I made myself very clear about my expectations."

"Put it on speakerphone," Gage whispered, his voice so quiet that I had to rely on reading his lips to understand what he said.

I nodded and did as he asked, hating the tears that were already burning my eyes.

"Something unexpected came up, and I had to leave. It was a family emergency," I said quietly, praying that Daisy wouldn't hear this conversation.

"You should have told me. I would have gone with you and helped you."

"I didn't want to bother you with it."

I struggled to keep my tone soft because what I really wanted to do was scream at him and rip him a new one for all of the stress and trauma he'd created for me. I wanted to yell from the top of the mountain and tell him every single thing I'd come to hate about him.

"Well, that's where you would be wrong. It wouldn't have been a bother. Imagine my frustration when I found out you left in the middle of the night, right after you promised me you wouldn't. Can you understand my worry that something terrible might have happened to you? To Daisy?"

I covered my mouth to keep from throwing up at the sound of my daughter's name coming out of his mouth.

"What do you want, Joel?" I asked, getting to the point as my voice broke.

"Oh, Julie. I thought I had already made that clear. I want what's mine. The only thing I've ever wanted was you. And in case you haven't noticed—I always get what I want."

"I'm not yours. I will never be yours," I bit out with a strangled sob.

"See, that's where you're wrong again. But I get it. It's hard being out on your own, trying to navigate a scary world while taking care of your daughter. You've done a great job with it, especially with handling that snowstorm you got caught in on your way up to that cabin."

I covered my mouth tighter with my trembling hand as the tears rushed down my cheeks. Gage watched me carefully as his jaw clenched and his fists balled at his sides. I wouldn't be surprised if Joel had put a tracking device on my car, in addition to the one he put in Uni, to keep track of where I went. However, I hadn't had the time or the knowledge to look for one before I left.

"It must be scary being out in the middle of nowhere with no one to hear you scream for help. No one would even notice if you truly went missing. How terrifying it must be to feel someone watching you, but never know exactly where they are."

My throat burned as bile rose from my stomach. He was a fucking monster.

"I won't keep you on here for long. I wouldn't want you to burn dinner," Joel said dismissively.

My heart stopped in my chest as the color drained from my face. If he knew that we were making dinner, then that meant he could see inside the house. I pressed a trembling finger to my lips to keep from screaming.

"Oh, and Julie?"

There was a long, silent pause that made the entire room go quiet as he waited for me to respond.

"Yeah," I replied as steadily as I could.

"I would be careful about leaving your daughter around a rottweiler. They're known to be an aggressive breed. They can turn on children in an instant, and we wouldn't want anything bad to happen to our sweet Daisy, now would we?"

Before I could say anything, the line went dead, leaving me in a stunned silence.

Just then, my phone rang again. I glanced down to see Patrick's name on the screen, but couldn't move. Gage grabbed it and answered it, holding it between his ear and shoulder as he wrapped his arms protectively around me.

"Yeah. We have a big fucking problem. Forget Plan A. We're moving to Plan B."

Ten

Joel

What a fucking idiot.

I sat back in my chair and watched the scene play out on the monitor as the camera in Julie's apartment was activated. It had been two days since I'd called her, so I was surprised it took her brother this long to get to town. Their parents were with him, all swooping in as if they were the CIA storming a criminal's secret lair. What they didn't know was that not only had I been expecting them, I had left a few surprises for them to find once they got there.

It was all so predictable, which was, to say the least, anticlimactic. While I missed being able to watch Julie any time I wanted, I was relieved that they hadn't found the secret camera that I had embedded in the unicorn as well. I was shocked that they let Daisy have it after removing the AirTag, and was relieved that the camera had gone undetected. It was already proving to be worth the investment so I could watch that asshole she was staying with and make sure he didn't try anything with her. I hadn't told her that I had seen him because I wanted to get her where I knew it mattered the most—her daughter.

I clicked on the screen that showed the camera in the unicorn and pressed the button to view the live feed. I knew that I couldn't rely on the battery lasting long now that I didn't have access to her apartment to change it out when needed. But I also couldn't stop myself from watching what she was doing and taking note of her location. While I didn't love the fact that someone was there with her, I felt confident that I could eliminate him just as easily as I had her husband.

The living room came into view as Daisy sat on the couch, coloring while the dog laid on the floor beside her. She was such a good child, and I knew she would adjust easily to me being her new dad once I got all this nonsense taken care of. It provided me with a great sense of relief, being able to see what was going on without being there by watching whenever I wanted to. The only downside was when Daisy would toss the stuffed animal around, and the only view I could get was of the wall or the couch cushion.

I had gone through a lot of work getting everything set up one day while Julie was at the store. I knew when she started acting differently that she was going to run—and honestly, I had been expecting it. When I made the first move on her, I was quite disappointed that she hadn't felt the same way, but I chalked it up to the fact that it was her first relationship since her husband died, and that she just needed time.

But then she started pulling away and getting more distant—so drastic times called for drastic measures. I had already put in a lot of time and effort into making this work, so I wasn't going to give up now.

When I noticed her spending more on groceries but not

having anything extra in her apartment, I figured she was stocking up so she could leave. I pretended not to notice and used the time she was gone to plant the cameras in her apartment and to set up the camera in the unicorn on her phone's network, so I didn't have to worry about where she went. I even went so far as to label it as our work Wi-Fi network so she wouldn't be suspicious.

Everything was going according to plan.

I smiled as I looked at the wall beside me, which was covered in photos of Julie from the first time I saw her, almost six years ago. She was at a coffee shop, consumed by the book she was reading, her features changing as the story unfolded. Her swollen stomach barely fit in the booth, but she was radiant and glowed the way only an expectant mother could.

I hadn't meant to stare at her and watch her, but I found that I couldn't look away. I pulled up the camera on my phone and started taking pictures, never knowing that this would become my new obsession.

She looked so happy that her eyes sparkled with joy. The only problem was that asshole husband of hers who stood in our way. I had considered cutting him out of the photos, but decided to leave him so it would be my motivation to finish what I started.

I shifted in my seat and returned my focus to Julie's apartment as her brother packed things into a duffel bag and looked around the room. Suddenly, his eyes landed on the picture frame where I'd hidden one of the cameras. I watched as he walked through the apartment, finding the rest of them. His face contorted with anger as he picked each one up and disabled it. I growled under my breath, frustrated even though I knew Julie wasn't coming back to this apartment.

Then he walked over to the table where her computer was and stopped, staring at the papers I'd left out for him to find. His face turned red as he gripped them tightly. He hadn't found the last camera yet, so I turned up the volume so I could hear what he was saying as his parents came into the room.

"What's that?" her mother asked, her brows furrowed as he turned the papers to face her.

"Adoption paperwork for Daisy. This fucking idiot is out of his god damn mind if he thinks Julie would ever sign off on this," he responded bitterly.

I tried to ignore the anger that was bubbling up to the surface because I knew he didn't mean that. Julie would sign them because I would make sure she did. One way or another, I was going to have her, and Daisy would be a bonus, given that I'd always wanted children.

"You need to see this," her dad said, covering his mouth with his hand.

They walked over, and I watched as they all stared in disbelief.

I had taken the photos out of Julie's album that she had made for Daisy with pictures of her with her father. Instead of cutting Mike out of the photos, I'd glued my head on top of his, so it was me and Daisy in the photos. I even added a few that had Julie, so they could see what a happy family the three of us would be.

"This asshole is sick," her father said, shaking his head.

"That's not the worst part," her mother said, holding up the heart-shaped keychain that was sitting beside them on the kitchen table. "This is the keychain that Julie bought for Mike the first Christmas they spent together. After his accident, they returned his belongings to her, and I remember her searching frantically for the keychain. She was devastated. We even went to the site of the accident, praying it would somehow show up."

"How did it get here?" her father asked, studying the mom.

"I don't know."

"Maybe Julie had another one made to replace it?" her father offered.

"No. I can't imagine Julie doing that," her mother rushed out. "She wouldn't have done something like that."

"Can I see it?" her brother asked, holding his hand out.

Her mother nodded and handed it to him. On the front of the heart, it was engraved with "I will love you forever," and on the back, it was engraved with "Julie + Mike."

He flipped it over, and I grinned when I watched his face change when he read what I had carved into the back of the heart after putting a line through Mike's name: You were mine first.

"What does that mean?" her mother asked, covering her mouth as a gasp slipped out.

"I think he's been obsessed with Julie longer than we thought."

"How did he get the keychain, though?" her dad asked.

"I don't think we want to know the answer to that question," her brother said, his eyes landing on the picture frame where the last camera was hidden.

"Why don't you guys take this stuff down, and I'll meet you outside in a few minutes," he said, continuing to stare at it.

Once they left the apartment, he picked up the picture frame and held it in front of his face.

"You picked the wrong fucking person to stalk, mother fucker," he growled. "When I find you—you're dead."

Eleven
Julie

I hadn't been calm in days, and I felt like I was going to go
out of my mind any minute from the anxiety threatening
to boil over. The worst of the storm had happened, but it
would still be days before they got anyone out to clear the
roads, which sucked because I really needed to get out of
the house and get some fresh air.

Daisy sat at the table, finishing her breakfast, while Gage
leaned against the island and drank his coffee as he studied
me.

"Stop it," I hissed as I walked past him and opened the
fridge.

I wasn't hungry but needed something to distract me. I
looked around, trying to force myself to think about what
I wanted to make for dinner. But the thought of food made
my already upset stomach more queasy, so I closed the door
and leaned against it.

"Mama, are we going to decorate for Christmas?" Daisy
asked, pulling my head out of the intrusive thoughts I was
having and making my heart sink.

I had been so consumed by everything with Joel that I had completely forgotten about Christmas. My eyes welled with tears as I stumbled for the right words to say, because how do you break a five-year-old's heart by telling them that you don't have anything to decorate with? I hadn't even had a chance to do any shopping, which meant that we didn't have gifts to exchange, nor did I have anything for Santa to leave for her.

Fuck. I was a terrible mother and was going to ruin Christmas for her.

"I was actually going to talk to you girls this morning to see if you wouldn't mind helping me decorate the house," Gage said, his smile sending calming energy through the room as it washed over me. "My grandmother loved decorating, so we have a ton of stuff."

"Can we help him?" Daisy asked, looking at me with the biggest smile and eyes filled with hope.

"Of course, my love. I think that would be so much fun!"

"Yay! I'm all done with breakfast. Can we start now?"

"Ummm…" I hesitated, not sure how to respond.

"I need to grab the stuff from the garage, but while I do that, why don't we put some Christmas music on?" Gage said, setting his coffee down on the island and walking with Daisy into the living room.

I stood there trying to pull myself together as I watched him pull Spotify up on the TV and search for Christmas music. Once it started playing, Daisy grinned as she danced around Duke, who didn't seem bothered in the least. She picked up the stuffed unicorn and held it with her as she danced in circles, having the time of her life.

Gage walked over, smiling at her over his shoulder as he stepped into the kitchen and pinned me against the fridge. His hand rested on my hip as his other hand gently brushed against my cheek with a tenderness that made my heart ache.

"You're not a terrible mom," he said so matter-of-factly that it felt like my heart was going to crack inside of my ribs and shatter with everything else.

"How do you do that?" I asked with a heavy sigh, letting my shoulders fall.

"Do what?"

"Get inside of my head and know exactly what I'm thinking and feeling."

"I just know you, Julie. I have for a while now. You can't blame yourself for things that have been out of your control. Keeping you guys safe has been the most important thing, so give yourself some grace that you don't have stuff ready for Christmas. We will figure it out together."

"But I don't even have a single gift," I said, lowering my face as I tried to hide the tears that threatened to spill over.

"Julie, we will figure it out together," he repeated more firmly as he gave my side a gentle squeeze and pressed a kiss to my forehead. "There are pastries on the counter. Eat something and have some coffee so we can get started with all of the fun we're going to have with decorating the house!"

His voice got purposely louder as he grinned at Daisy, who was now holding the unicorn, pointing it at us as she swayed with the music. Her face was so incredibly beautiful, but it was the smile that radiated pure happiness that made my heart swell. Maybe I wasn't doing everything wrong after all.

<u>Twelve</u>
Gage

I was on pins and needles waiting for the big surprise to happen as we continued decorating the house. The tree that my grandmother loved so much was set up in the entryway of the house, where it always went every year. There was glitter everywhere from all of the ornaments and the strands of ribbon that Daisy insisted on using for the bottom half of the tree, but none of that bothered me when I saw how happy she was.

Julie hadn't stopped smiling once we got started, and I loved watching her and Daisy as they laughed constantly and worked together to make the tree as beautiful as possible. What they didn't know was that they could simply stand in front of the tree and it would be the most beautiful thing I had ever seen.

We'd worked our way through putting out all of the Christmas knick-knacks, and Daisy squealed when we found the Santa and Mrs. Claus cookie jars. Julie promised that they would make cookies together soon, provided she had all the ingredients. While the roads hadn't been cleared yet, there wasn't anything that would stop me from putting my truck in four-wheel drive and making a run to the store to get supplies.

Just as they were finishing hanging the stockings by the fireplace, the doorbell rang.

Julie jumped and whipped around, pure terror on her face as she wrapped her arms around Daisy protectively while Duke barked loudly.

Fuck. I should have thought this through and told her about the surprise before it happened. I hadn't stopped to think that she would think the worst was happening with an unexpected visitor, especially given that Joel seemed to know so much about where she was staying.

"It's okay," I assured her quickly, holding my hands in front of me. "It's a good surprise. I promise."

She nodded her head, but I could see that she was still holding her breath as she waited for me to open the door. I leaned up and looked through the peephole, just to be sure.

"It's freezing balls out here, you asshole. Open the door," Patrick muttered on the other side.

I rolled my eyes, somewhat relieved that he seemed back to his old self instead of the person who was insistent on kicking my ass the last time I saw him.

I slowly pulled the door open and stepped back, allowing them to enter.

"Merry Christmas!" Patrick said, coming inside and pushing his suitcase to the side as Daisy squealed and went running to him.

He dropped to his knees and opened his arms, locking her in a tight hug.

"Oh my gosh!" Julie exclaimed, walking over right as I opened the door further to reveal her parents.

"Mom! Dad! What are you guys doing here?" Julie rushed over and pulled both of her parents into a hug as I pushed the door closed behind them to keep the snow and cold air from coming inside.

"I told you that we wanted to spend Christmas together," Patrick said as he set Daisy down, who was already jumping into the arms of her grandparents. "Merry Christmas, Jules."

Julie wiped at the tears on her face as she stepped to the side and hugged her brother. My heart felt like it was going to burst from all of the emotions surrounding me, especially when I knew how long it had been since they'd spent Christmas together.

"I can't believe you guys are here," Julie said as she stepped back, continuing to wipe her eyes. "This is just… It's so…. Oh my God, I can't even speak right now."

She shook her head and turned into Patrick's shoulder as he squeezed her comfortingly.

"The house looks wonderful," Lynn, her mother, said as she stepped inside and let Daisy show her the tree. "It reminds me so much of the time we spent up here during the holidays with your grandparents. Your grandmother would have loved this. Thank you so much for inviting us, it's so good to see you again." She smiled warmly at me and patted my shoulder, but it had been far too long since I'd seen her, so I pulled her in for a hug I hadn't realized just how bad I needed. She squeezed me tightly, both of us not saying the things we wanted to say while Daisy waited impatiently for her so she could continue her tour.

"I'm going to go see what we have for dinner," Julie said, happily looking around the room at her family.

"Sounds good. I'll help you in a few. Why don't I show you guys the bedroom options, and we can get everyone settled in?" I offered, glancing between Patrick and his parents.

"Can we have a sleepover in your bedroom tonight?" Daisy asked Lynn, pulling at her arm as she pleaded with her eyes.

"Of course, my love. I would love nothing more," Lynn responded before looking at me. "Is there any chance you still have the bedroom with three beds in it?"

"I do." I grinned and nodded my head for them to follow me after I grabbed their luggage and started down the hallway.

While we had the entire upstairs available, I hadn't had a chance to go through any of those rooms yet and felt better having Julie's family close to me, just in case they needed anything.

Thirteen
Julie

I covered my mouth with my hand to keep from spitting food across the table as I struggled to control my laughter. Patrick's eyes lit up as he told Daisy the story about the time we came to the inn for Christmas one year, and I was so hungry that I ate all of the popcorn from the strands we had made to decorate the tree.

"In all fairness, your mom was about your age, if not a little younger," Dad said with a dimpled smile as he looked down at Daisy, who was nestled between him and my mother.

I loved how much she loved her grandparents and hated how long it had been since we'd seen them. While they came to visit us whenever they could, things had been different after Mike died.

"No one told me we couldn't eat it," I replied, holding my hands up.

"It's partly why I didn't offer to make popcorn earlier," Gage teased, giving me a wink that sent a jolt straight between my thighs. "I wasn't sure I could trust your mom not to eat it again."

"Mommy," Daisy said with a sigh as she pressed her little hand dramatically to her forehead. "You were so silly!"

I shrugged, loving how happy she was.

She grinned, but it was quickly erased as a big yawn pulled across her face instead.

"Looks like it will be an early night tonight," I said softly, watching her as she fought the tiredness that was washing over her. We had been up early, and it was a busy day filled with fun and unexpected surprises.

"I'm not tired," she objected, looking nervously up at my mother.

"I was thinking that maybe we could watch a movie in our bedroom tonight," my mom said softly to her. We all knew that a few minutes into the movie, Daisy would be out cold. "I saw a TV in there. We could cuddle up together and watch a Christmas one."

"Yeah! Let's do that!" Daisy's sudden burst of excitement temporarily disturbed Duke as he lifted his head to see what was happening before returning it to the floor as he went back to sleep. Glitter had covered the majority of the house, not even sparing Duke, as the top of his head glistened in the light.

"Well, if you guys want to go start getting everything set up for your movie night, I'll get the table cleared and then come say goodnight," I said, pushing away from the table.

"I'll help you clean up," Gage offered, not looking the least bit bothered by the look my brother gave him.

"Thanks," I replied as I started collecting the dishes from the table and ignored the tension building in the room as my parents took Daisy to their room, leaving Patrick alone with us.

"I don't like whatever this is," Patrick said, his voice turning into the one I hated when I was a kid.

"You don't like what exactly?" I asked, turning to face him with a hand on my hip.

"Don't act like I'm stupid, Jules. Everyone can see something is going on between the two of you."

"Are you fucking kidding me?" I felt Gage step beside me and knew that no matter what happened with my brother, I had his support. "Nothing is happening between us other than he's keeping me and your niece safe from some asshole who is stalking me. Get your shit together, Patrick, or I swear to God…"

"You swear to God what, Jules?"

"I've gone a long time doing this on my own, so don't think for a second that I won't help you pack your shit and kick you out. Whatever this crap is between you and Gage is between you and Gage. Leave me the hell out of it and mind your own business. If you came down here to fight with him or accuse us of something, then you can leave."

"I came because I was worried about you. I wanted to help. And I wasn't lying when I said that it would be great to spend Christmas together as a family," Patrick said, his tone softening some.

"Then act like it," I bit out, letting my emotions from the past few days get the better of me. "I don't need any additional stress right now, Pat. I have enough on my plate as it is, so if you're here to make things harder for me—"

"That's not my intention. I'm sorry. I just thought I saw something between the two of you, and I guess I just… I don't know. It triggered something inside of me." Pat held his hands up and gave me an apologetic look.

"So what if there is something between us?" Gage asked, leaning against the counter with his ankles crossed and his arms folded over his chest.

Why did he not know when to shut up? I didn't need them fighting over anything right now.

"Are you saying there is?" Patrick pushed, mimicking Gage's rigid pose.

Gage shrugged, but I noticed the way his jaw ticked as he stared at my brother.

"We had an agreement," Patrick said sharply.

"Yeah, when we were eighteen. Things change."

"So it seems."

I didn't miss the way Patrick's words were laced with venom, but my mind was racing as I tried to keep up.

"What agreement?" I asked, looking between the two of them.

What felt like minutes went by without anyone speaking, forcing me to raise my eyebrows and stare at them until one of them gave in.

"We made an agreement that you were off limits," Patrick said, looking from Gage to me.

"I'm sorry—what?"

"When we were eighteen, we made an agreement that you were off limits," Patrick repeated.

"Why?"

"Because you were my little sister, and I didn't want to see you get hurt. I knew that Gage had a way with getting whatever he wanted from girls, and I didn't want that for you. So, we made an agreement that you were off limits."

"Oh my God," I muttered with a heavy sigh as I pressed a finger against my temple and rubbed it. "Pat, we're not kids anymore. I'm not some sixteen-year-old girl who needs her brother to protect her from his friends. I'm thirty-six years old with a child, for God's sake!"

"That doesn't mean that I don't worry about you, Jules. You think you know him, but you don't," Patrick objected.

"Really? We're going to go there?" Gage said, his eyes narrowing.

"What? You don't want my sister to know what you did?"

Patrick turned to face Gage again, taking a few steps until they were standing chest to chest as Gage pushed off from the counter.

"Do you even know what I did? Or are you still going by what Melanie told you?" Gage cocked his head to the side as he stared at my brother.

"Fuck you. I told you not to ever speak her name again," Patrick growled as I stepped out of the way.

I had no idea what was going on, but I knew this wasn't going to end well.

"And I told you to go fuck yourself if you think you have any control over what I do."

"Like fuck my fiancée?" Patrick spat out, making me flinch.

My eyes widened in horror as I looked past Patrick to Gage, whose jaw tightened as he glanced at me. All it took was that split second of being distracted for Patrick to land a blow as his fist made contact with Gage's eye.

I gasped and stepped out of the way as Gage threw a punch at Patrick, hitting him in the ribs. Before I knew it, they were both going at it with fists flying and curse words louder than the dishes they had knocked to the ground.

A few minutes later, my father came storming into the room, the vein in his forehead protruding as he looked at the mess they'd made in a matter of seconds.

"What in the world has gotten into you two?" he scolded, looking at them as they stepped away and wiped the blood from their faces.

I covered my mouth with my hands and stared in disbelief.

"Your mother is trying to get Daisy settled in, and the last thing she needs to see is all of this bullshit. You two get this cleaned up right now. Julie, come say goodnight to your daughter."

I nodded as my dad shook his head at the guys and stormed out as quickly as he came in.

I could feel both of them watching me as I stepped over the broken glass and walked away, not bothering to look back.

Fourteen
Gage

"I didn't fuck Melanie," I said, needing to get it off my chest as I swept the broken glass into a pile and grabbed the dustpan. "You know I would never do that to you."

"Then why did she insist that you did?" He pushed the chairs out of the way so I could sweep under the table. I would still need to mop and vacuum to make sure we got all the glass cleaned up so Daisy wouldn't step on it.

"Because I caught her fucking Anthony two months before your wedding. When she knew that I knew, she tried to manipulate me into not telling you. She said that she would give me whatever I wanted to keep quiet, and when I refused, she said that she would destroy our friendship before she allowed me to ruin her marriage."

Patrick's back was to me as he moved the chairs back under the table, holding onto one as he kept his head down.

"Why didn't you say something?"

"Because I was stupid and gave her the opportunity to tell you herself. But when she didn't, I knew that I had missed my window and that you weren't going to believe me, no matter what I said."

Patrick turned around and faced me, his jaw clenched as he shook his head.

"She said that you forced yourself on her and that she was tipsy, so she didn't realize what was happening until it was too late. Then, when I saw you, you were acting all weird and avoiding her."

"Because I already knew what she had said. She threatened me with it beforehand and told me that if I said anything about her fucking Anthony, she would make my life a living hell. She wanted me out of your life so her secret would stay safe."

Patrick inhaled deeply and scrubbed a hand down his face.

"Did anything actually happen between you two? And don't fucking lie. Just tell me the truth, once and for all."

"The fact that you even have to ask that shows what you think about me. About our friendship," I said, feeling the hurt deep inside of my chest. "You should know that I would never do that to you. Drunk or not—I would never do that to someone I cared for, nor would I ever force myself onto anyone."

Patrick arched an eyebrow. "Cared as in past tense?"

"You chose her over me. A girl you hadn't known long enough to make that kind of judgment call. You let her come between us and fill your head with lies. You believed her over someone who had been there for you from the very start. So yeah, Patrick cared. A lot has changed between us, and I don't know that we can just sweep this under the rug and move on."

"Just like I don't know that I can just look the other way

and pretend that I don't know you're interested in my sister."

I put the broom away and stood in front of him as I let out a heavy sigh.

"When it comes to Julie, I will always do everything I can to protect her and keep her safe. I will not let anything happen to her. But I'm also done sitting on the sidelines, pretending that I haven't had feelings for her for over twenty years. I don't know what to tell you, but as far as your sister is concerned, I don't give a fuck what you think."

"Careful," he warned, anger flashing in his eyes.

"Or what? You'll sucker punch me again?" I narrowed my eyes as I looked him up and down. "You still hit like a little bitch."

Patrick's nostrils flared, but before he could speak, Julie walked in.

"I really hate to break up whatever lovers' quarrel this is that you guys are still having, but Daisy wants to say goodnight to her uncle," Julie said with an exhausted sigh as she held the stuffed unicorn in her hands.

Patrick nodded, giving me a final glare before walking past and shoulder-checking me on the way.

"Man, he really doesn't get over things, does he?" Julie said after he left the room. "I thought I held grudges, but Pat deserves like a medal or something for how long he can hold one."

I chuckled, and my body began to relax.

"What's up with Uni? Did she forget to take it to their room?"

"No, she wanted me to keep it so I wasn't lonely tonight. So I'm officially on Uni duty for the night."

"Are you heading to bed right away?" I asked, feeling my palms start to sweat as my nerves skyrocketed.

I'd been wanting some alone time with Julie for a while now, and since Daisy was having a sleepover with her grandparents, it seemed it was now or never.

"Probably not. I'm still a little wired from the day and need some time to decompress."

"It's probably those eight cups of coffee you had," I teased, loving how she'd allowed me to make her fancy coffee when she got too frustrated to figure out how to use the coffee maker.

"Hey—that was good coffee," she said, pointing a finger at me. "You should open a coffee shop. You would totally rock that and would have a line out the door."

"I don't think my coffee skills are that great."

"Maybe not, but you'd still have a line out the door regardless because who wouldn't want to watch a hot, tatted-up guy make their coffee?"

I was still processing her words when I noticed the faint blush that turned her cheeks red as her eyes widened when she realized what she said.

"Did you just call me hot?" I chewed the side of my lip as I watched her squirm.

"No? Yes? I don't know…" She looked around the kitchen, but I kept my gaze on her. "I mean, come on, it's not like you don't know that you're hot. It's not like I'm not stating the obvious."

I licked my lips, the grin stretching my cheeks as I watched her reaction to it. Fuck. Everything she did was a turn on for me, and I wasn't going to be able to keep my attraction to her contained much longer.

"Why don't you bring Uni and come watch a movie with me?" I offered, hoping she would take me up on it.

"Here on the couch?"

There was a nervousness in her tone as she looked past the couch and down the hall to where my room was.

The house was large, with rooms on both sides of the house. It just so happened that my room and the room she had been using with Daisy were on one side of the house, while all of the others were on the other side.

"No," I said, shaking my head. Her heated gaze met mine, sending a jolt right through me. "I thought maybe we could watch one in my room if you want to. No pressure."

She pulled her lower lip between her teeth and smiled.

"I would love to."

I didn't bother hiding my grin as I placed my hand on her lower back and guided her toward my room. A door at the other end of the hallway opened, and Patrick stepped out, just as Julie walked into my room. I gave him a nod and then smirked as I stepped inside and closed the door behind me.

Fifteen

Julie

I was in Gage's room. A room that smelled very much like the man I had been struggling to keep my hands off of from the moment I stepped through the door and forced myself into his life. A man who laid comfortably on the bed beside me, propped up with a pillow as he watched a movie that I had no idea what it was because all I could focus on was the way his ripped abs looked under the t-shirt that pulled tightly across them.

I glanced around the room, looking for something— anything to take my mind off of the intense attraction I felt toward him. Uni sat on the dresser beneath the TV mounted to the wall, and I knew it was judging me. So what if it were just a stuffed animal? If it had human emotions, the one it would be feeling right now would be judgment for me wanting to hump my brother's former best friend.

I didn't even want to get started on that subject, given how they hadn't been able to be around each other more than a few hours before they got into a physical fight. Christmas was going to be rocky, to say the least, and both would likely be sporting black eyes and fat lips for the special day. I looked up at Gage, noticing the swelling had started to go down, but then

I got distracted by the flecks of gold in his eyes.

As if knowing what I was thinking, he lowered his eyes and looked at me, giving me a warm smile.

"It looks worse than it is," he said softly.

"I hate that you guys are still fighting," I admitted, though I was too tired to try to get into any of that at the moment.

"It'll be fine. We'll get through it. And just for the record, I didn't fuck Melanie. That was a lie she started when I caught her sleeping with someone else."

"Did you tell him that?"

"No. But only because I knew he wouldn't listen. I tried telling him earlier tonight, and he still didn't believe me."

I nodded because I didn't know what else to say. His fight with my brother had been going on for so long now that I didn't understand why they hadn't just talked about it and figured things out. Especially after Melanie called off their engagement. I trusted Gage, not just because I had feelings for him, but because I never liked or trusted Melanie. I could absolutely see her trying to come between them and making Gage the bad guy.

"How are you feeling?" he asked, changing the subject.

I shrugged, unsure of how to answer that as I sank lower into his pillow, which caused it to make the air smell like him. I groaned quietly and tried to fight the urge to stick my face in it and continue inhaling it until I passed out. It should be illegal to smell that good.

"Fine, I guess," I replied when I realized he was still waiting for an answer. "I know it's only been a little over a week that we've been here with you, but it feels like time is just flying by. Christmas will be here before we know it, and I'm not in the least bit ready for it."

"I know. But I promise, we'll get some shopping done this weekend. The roads should be better so we can head into town and get some stuff done."

"Do you really think the roads will be clear by then?"

"More or less. I mean, they weren't too bad for your brother and parents to make it up here."

I nodded but chewed my lip to keep from saying what was really worrying me. If my family could get to the cabin easily, so could Joel. Given that we didn't find the AirTag until we were already up there, it also meant that he had our exact location.

"Nothing is going to happen to you, Julie. I promise," he said softly as he rolled onto his side and tucked a strand of hair behind my ear.

My eyes fluttered at the contact, and I closed my eyes, wishing this could be more.

"I really wish I could believe that," I admitted quietly, slowly opening my eyes to find his watching me. "He's a dangerous man. I don't know what he's capable of at this point. He knows where I'm at. He was somehow able to see inside the house. What's to stop him from coming for me?"

"Me. I will stop him. So will Patrick and your dad. We've got you protected. I promise. This house is as secure as Fort Knox. No one is coming or going without me knowing. I don't know how he saw inside the house, but I can guarantee you that he's not here. We scanned for more

AirTags, so there aren't any more tracking devices either."

"I know," I said, sucking in a deep breath. "I just wish I knew where he was and what he wanted."

"Well, we know what he wants," Gage said quietly with a sadness to his voice. "But he's not going to get it."

"It looks like no one is going to get what they want," I teased, not thinking through my words before I said them.

A heat flashed in his eyes as he stared at me.

"What do you want, Julie?"

I slowly exhaled, making sure I wanted to go through with it before I said anything. But that was the thing with Gage, I didn't have to question it. I'd known I wanted him since the summer I turned sixteen and he seemed to hang around the inn more than usual.

"You," I whispered, licking my lips as I watched his emotions flicker across his face.

"Well, that I can make happen."

He slowly leaned forward, watching my reaction as his lips feathered over mine. My heart hammered in my chest as I reached up and wrapped my hand behind his neck, pulling him closer to me. I rolled onto my back, dragging him along with me until his body was lying on top of mine.

I parted my lips and caressed his with my tongue, loving the way he groaned and swiped his tongue across mine. He deepened the kiss as he held himself slightly above me, not putting his full weight on me. My back arched as we kissed, his hand skimming along my side. I wanted him to touch me more as the ache between my thighs started to build.

His hand slid up, caressing my breast as he shoved the fabric of my shirt up and exposed my stomach. I opened my thighs wider, allowing him to settle between them as I started to feel the outline of his erection.

I whimpered and started grinding my hips against him, desperate for any friction I could get. I heard him start to chuckle as he pulled away and looked at me.

"Are you sure you want to do this?" he asked, his hand resting on my side again.

"Yes. Very sure. Like so sure that if you don't start removing clothes and touching my body, I'm going to climb on top of you and hump your leg until I get off," I warned.

He raised an eyebrow and grinned, his face looking beyond beautiful.

"Well, we wouldn't want that to happen, now would we?" he teased, lifting himself to his knees as he stayed between my thighs.

"I don't know. I'm pretty worked up already, so I don't really care what I have to hump as long as I get a release."

He licked his lips and then slowly reached behind and pulled his shirt over his head before tossing it to the floor.

I stared at his perfect body as I got wetter thinking about all of the things I wanted to do to it. We were both wearing too many clothes for what I needed to happen.

"Lift your hips," he said, nodding to them.

I did as he asked and lifted them while he grabbed the waistband of my leggings and pulled them down my body, taking my panties with them. My instinct was to immediately shut my legs and not let him see me like this, but the way he looked at my body made me want to open up for him and let him do whatever he wanted.

"Fuck, Julie," he moaned, chewing his lip as he trailed a finger along my seam, making me jump. "Not only is this pussy perfect, but look how wet she is for me already."

I gripped the sheets and held on as he slowly slid his finger along it again, this time slipping it inside and making me gasp. My body was on fire and ready for him to bring me immense amounts of pleasure.

"Can I?" he asked, looking down at my pussy as he continued finger fucking it.

"I don't know what the question is, but the answer is yes. Whatever makes me come, yes."

He chuckled again and then lowered himself between my legs, taking his time as he kissed the inside of my thighs, slowly licking the arousal from his fingers as he removed them. I was about to complain about it, but then he spread me wide with his hands and slid his tongue between my lips, and I no longer knew how to speak.

My back arched as he gripped my thighs, keeping them open while he devoured my pussy like it was his last meal. He was driving me crazy as he alternated between licking and kissing, and then started sucking my clit. I knew I wasn't going to last long when he stuck two fingers inside and pressed on my G-spot while flicking my clit with his tongue.

Within seconds, I covered my mouth to keep from screaming as my pussy spasmed around him, coming harder than I'd ever come before.

Once I was done, he slowly pulled away and watched me as he casually wiped the corners of his mouth with his fingers.

"You tasted just as good as I thought you would," he said as he climbed off the bed and finished undressing. "Now I need to see if she grips my cock the same way she gripped my fingers."

"Fuck. Yes, please," I replied with a sigh as I tried to catch my breath.

"How do you want it?" he asked as he stroked himself, distracting me with his monster cock.

"I want it however you want it."

He tore open a condom with his teeth, then sheathed himself as he climbed back onto the bed.

"Do you want to ride my cock and make yourself come again?"

I nodded, pulling my lip between my teeth.

He grinned and laid down sideways across the bed so I didn't have to go far to straddle him. My body felt nice and relaxed, but I wasn't sure I had the strength to ride him the way I wanted to. He waited as I climbed on top of him and held my hips steady as I slowly lowered myself onto his cock, wincing at the sting as he stretched me fuller than I'd ever been before.

"Fuck," I moaned, letting my head fall back.

"Seeing you like this, with your tits begging to be sucked while you sit on my cock makes me want to come already."

I nodded because I was ready to come again as well. I

waited a few seconds and then sank lower until he was fully seated inside of me.

"You're so big," I whimpered, slowly moving my hips as I got used to the fullness.

He didn't say anything as he leaned forward and pulled a puckered nipple into his mouth, sucking it so hard that it bordered on pain but was quickly replaced with pleasure. I closed my eyes and began riding him the way I'd always wanted to.

I shifted slightly, making his shaft line up with my clit and began bouncing hard and fast, feeling the tingle up my spine. His hands gripped my hips tightly and held me as he bucked up from beneath me, hitting my G-spot with every thrust while stimulating my clit at the same time.

"FUCK!" I cried out, not bothering to stop myself this time as a mind-blowing orgasm ripped through me, followed by his a few seconds later.

I panted and tried to catch my breath as he wrapped his arms around me and pulled me to his chest. I just slept with my brother's former best friend, and I didn't have a single regret about it.

<u>Sixteen</u>
Joel

My fist slammed down onto the rickety wooden table in the motel room as I stared at my phone. I had the app pulled up so I could watch the live video from the unicorn camera and see what they were up to. What I hadn't expected to see was Julie riding that asshole as she fucked him. I let out a deep growl as my jaw tightened, the urge to go there and kill the mother fucker for touching my woman almost unbearable.

I knew that there would be a time when Julie would move on and forget about her dead husband, but the guy she was supposed to move on with was me. I had put in the time and energy to give her the life that she needed long before I ever killed Mike. Everything I did was a calculated move, including his car accident, and the life I created for her and Daisy after he was gone. He wasn't a bad guy; he just made the mistake of being with the woman whom I loved and was destined to be with myself.

I watched as she closed her eyes and tipped her head back, the same way she looked the first night I had spied on her in her apartment. She didn't know about the hidden cameras, and at first, I was reluctant to put one in her bedroom because I didn't want to cross the line. But once I saw what she did and how she pleasured herself when Daisy was asleep, I couldn't stop myself. I was eager to watch her and learn what she liked so I would know how to take care of her when the time came. I wanted to bring her nothing but pleasure, much like the pleasure she brought to me every time I watched her masturbate and jacked myself off to the sight of her coming undone.

Julie was an immaculate woman and deserved only the best, which was why I was the person who would give that to her.

I just needed to deal with a few things before that could happen. I was so close to having her, and she didn't even know it, thanks to the AirTag that had given me their exact location before it was disabled.

Seventeen
Gage

"You have to sit still," Daisy said with a sigh as she held my hand on the pillow and looked at the nail polish she had painted my nails with. "I think it needs another coat."

"I think it might be good like it is," I replied, grinning when I saw her face scrunched in concentration. I not only had enough polish covering my nails, but I also had pink all along my fingers, and some had accidentally ended up on my hand when she dropped the brush.

"Okay. But let me file this nail. It's crooked and has a jagged edge."

I nodded and watched as she moved the glittery pink nail file along my nail, making it smooth and even.

"There. Perfect." She leaned back and studied her work with the biggest smile on her face.

"They look amazing, Daisy. Thank you for doing my nails for me," I said, loving the happiness still radiating on her face.

Julie was in the kitchen making breakfast with her mom while her dad was shoveling the snow out front. I insisted that I would do it, but he told me that it was good for him to be up and moving. Not only that, he needed some fresh air. I agreed, but made sure I sat where I could look out the floor-to-ceiling window to keep an eye on him. The storm had finally ended, which was a welcome relief, given the amount of snow we had already received.

"Good morning, Daisy," Patrick said as he came into the living room and smiled at her.

"Good morning, Uncle Pat. Do you want your nails painted?"

He frowned, unsure of how to answer as I watched him. He had a few bruises from our scuffle last night, but overall didn't look too bad. I had a black eye, but it was already starting to heal.

"Ummm… I don't…" he stuttered cautiously, his eyebrows rising as her shoulders fell in disappointment.

I lifted my hands and wiggled my fingers for him to see that she had already done mine, catching Julie smiling at us from the kitchen.

"I wasn't sure if you had enough polish left to do mine," he added quickly, nodding to me. "But it looks like Gage didn't use all of it after all. I would love for you to paint my nails, sweetheart."

She giggled and squirmed on the couch until she was turned around, facing him as he sat down.

I chuckled and got up, giving them some space. I knew how much he adored her and wanted them to have their time together.

"What can I help with?" I asked as I walked up behind Julie and skimmed my hand across her lower back. She let out a soft gasp that only I could hear as she turned and smiled at me. While I had vivid memories of last night, I had forgotten that no one else knew what had happened between us. I had no idea if she was ready for anyone to know, so I pulled my hand away and tried to act as normally as I could.

"Ummm…. I think we have everything covered. Would you mind making me some coffee?"

I nodded and grinned, feeling the weight of her mother's gaze on us as she watched us. Apparently, I hadn't been subtle at all.

"Espresso?" I asked, already knowing the answer because it was what I had made for her every morning since she had arrived. But I felt nervous and needed something to distract me.

"Yes, please."

"You got it." I grabbed one of the pods she liked and turned to Lynn. "Would you like coffee this morning?"

"That would be lovely. Thank you."

I grabbed the small rack that held a variety of flavored pods and set it down in front of her.

"Just let me know which one you'd like and I'll make it for you."

She smiled and nodded.

"I'll do espresso like Julie, please. I have a feeling I'm going to need a lot of caffeine today."

Julie turned around and frowned at her mother, a look of concern crossing her face.

"Did Daisy keep you up last night?" Julie asked, keeping her voice low so Daisy didn't hear.

"Oh, gosh, no. She was such a sweet girl and fell asleep right away. It was your dad who kept me up most of the night," Lynn said with a heavy sigh. "I swear, that man snores differently here than he does at home. At one point, it sounded like he was using a power drill. I didn't finally fall asleep until close to four this morning."

"I'm sorry it was such a late night for you. I'm glad it wasn't Daisy that kept you up, though," Julie said, turning to grab the dishes from the oven.

"It seems dad wasn't the only one making noises that kept everyone up last night," Patrick said dryly as he walked into the kitchen and pinned me with a look.

Julie spun around, her eyes wide and cheeks flushed, which totally gave us away.

I looked down and rubbed the back of my neck while the only sound in the room was the drizzle of coffee pouring into the cup.

"I thought I made myself clear about things between you and my sister," he said, his voice low as Daisy pulled out a chair and sat down at the kitchen table while Lynn helped her. Julie's dad had just come inside, his cheeks red from the blistery cold air outside.

I looked past Patrick to Julie, who looked slightly pale and worried.

"And I thought I made myself perfectly clear about things between me and your sister," I responded, closing the distance between us as I stepped into his space. "What happens between us is none of your fucking business, so stay the fuck out of it."

Patrick's nostrils flared as he shoved me hard, forcing me to take a few steps back.

"Stop it," Julie hissed, stepping in between us. "We don't have time for this bullshit, so both of you need to get your heads out of your asses and knock it off."

I worked my jaw back and forth as Patrick and I continued to stare at each other. But then Julie placed her hand on my arm and got my attention.

"Please," she whispered, her voice cracking with emotion.

"Of course. Anything for you."

I wanted to lean down and kiss her to show her that I meant what I said, but now wasn't the time or place for that. Instead, I finished making coffee for Julie and her mom, then joined the family at the long dining table that hadn't been used like this in so long, I couldn't remember the last time. After my grandfather passed away, my grandmother struggled to keep the inn up and running as the guests stopped coming and her income trickled to almost nothing.

My stomach knotted at the thought of clearing the place out and putting it up for sale, especially when I realized how much work they had put into making it one of the most magical places I had ever been to. I always chalked that feeling up to being young and not knowing any better, but as I looked around the table at the family before me, their happiness wasn't fake. It was as if the magic of the inn had seeped into all of them, making everyone forget about the danger that threatened to take all of it away.

<u>Eighteen</u>
Julie

The guys had decided to put up Christmas lights outside and had been out there for twenty minutes, as my mother and I sat on the couch and watched. Daisy had started to not feel well shortly after breakfast and had fallen asleep between us while Duke laid on the rug beneath her, always guarding her.

My dad held up a strand of lights and looked at it, while Patrick shook his head, folding his arms over his chest and scowling. Gage looked off to the side and lowered his head, clearly not wanting to get into another fight with my brother.

I chewed my thumbnail anxiously as I watched them, hating that there was still so much anger and hostility between them. I used to say that nothing would ever come between me and my brother, but my stomach soured at the thought as I looked at Gage and felt my heart flutter in my chest.

I knew it was wrong to get involved with him—especially right now. But it was damn near impossible not to when we were walking sticks of dynamite, trying to avoid the flames that burned so strongly between us. I spent my teen years and early twenties being obsessed with Gage, only to tell myself nothing could ever happen because he was my brother's best friend. Only things were different now, and I couldn't talk my heart out of loving him like I used to.

"If you keep chewing your nails like that, you won't have anything for her to paint when she wakes up," my mother said, nodding to Daisy.

"She really does love painting nails." I smiled and gently brushed a strand of hair off her face as she slept. "I can't believe she got all of the guys to let her paint theirs."

"Me neither. I can honestly say that I've never seen three manly men out there hanging Christmas lights with their pretty pink nails glistening in the sun," she teased.

"She's going to be so excited when she wakes up and sees the lights. I feel bad that Christmas has been off for her…" I let my voice trail as I realized that it was only a week and a half until Christmas, and I still didn't have anything figured out for gifts. Now that my parents and Patrick were there with us, I needed to have gifts for them too, which only added to the stress I was already feeling.

"Gage mentioned to your father that he thinks the roads will be clear enough to head into town soon," my mother said softly, staring out the window and smiling when she saw my dad pointing at both of the guys and frowning. "He really does love both of them like sons."

"How were the roads coming up here yesterday?" I asked, clearing my throat as I shifted the topic away from how Gage has always felt like family to us. I didn't need to think about him like that while still remembering the taste of his lips and how they felt trailing across my skin.

"Not too bad. A little icy here and there, but you know Patrick and his big truck. That thing can handle just about anything."

"That's good to know," I replied, not thinking through my answer before it slipped out.

There wasn't a time when I hadn't been thinking about what we would do if Joel showed up here. My main priority was keeping Daisy safe. Nothing else mattered. But part of keeping her safe meant that we had a way to get the hell out of here if needed, and quickly. While my car had done alright for the most part on our way up here, I felt better knowing that my brother's beast of a truck could save the day if needed.

My mind was racing, and before I could stop it, warning bells started flashing through my brain.

"Wait a minute—" I said, holding my hand up as my mother began to speak. "How did Patrick get his truck? I thought you guys flew into Seattle yesterday and rented a car to drive up to the inn?"

My mother's cheeks flushed crimson as she looked out the window for someone to save her from having this conversation with me. Patrick had left his truck at my apartment because I had two parking spaces included in my lease. Since I didn't need both, I told him he could use the other space to store his truck until he decided whether to sell it.

"You've got to be fucking kidding me," I growled, gently getting up off the couch so I didn't wake Daisy. I shook my head and stalked over to the front door, flinging it open as their heads all whipped in my direction.

Gage smiled warmly while my dad looked confused. My mother sat on the couch, covering her mouth with her hands as Patrick's eyes went straight to her.

I stepped into the cold, not caring that I didn't have a coat on. Thanks to my anger, I was burning up and didn't need one. I pulled the door closed and turned to Patrick, my eyes burning into his.

"What the fuck were you doing at my apartment yesterday?" I snarled, poking my finger into his chest as I stepped closer to him.

"I was handling what needed to be handled," he replied easily, tilting his head to the side as he studied me.

"I didn't need anything handled. Do you not remember our conversation about how dangerous this guy is? I don't need you putting yourself in danger!"

"I wasn't in danger."

I inhaled deeply, trying to force the oxygen to my brain so I could think clearly.

"You said it yourself that he was dangerous. What could you have possibly needed to handle by going there? You knew that Daisy and I were safe here!" I threw my hands up.

He stood straight, pulling his shoulders back as he cocked his head to the side and studied me. I hated it when he did this, always having to make sure I knew just how much bigger than me he was.

"I went to make a point," he said softly.

"A point? A point? Who were you making a point to? Me? Was this all some sort of power play that you needed to show up against Gage so he'd think you're tough and manly?"

"No. I went because I knew he was watching your apartment, and I wanted him to see exactly who he was going up against. No one—and I repeat no one—" he paused, looking at Gage, "fucks with my family. I walked out of the middle of a multi-million-dollar deal in New York, just to catch the first flight to Seattle so I could take care of things. You might be safe right now, but I won't rest until he's dealt with."

I pulled back, startled by his words as my lower lip trembled.

"What are you going to do?" I whispered, all of the anger from a few minutes ago rushing out of me.

"Whatever I have to. Make no mistake, I don't fuck around when it comes to my family, Jules. I don't care whose blood I have on my hands as long as you and Daisy are taken care of."

Nineteen
Gage

I knew Patrick hadn't told Julie what they'd found when they went to her apartment, which put me in an awkward spot, having to keep that secret from her. But we all agreed that it wasn't the right time to tell her and create more worry on top of everything else she had going on. Daisy had started not to feel well this morning, but on top of that, we'd discovered that someone had cut the lock off the shed out back. I hadn't had a chance to get to the shed since I'd arrived, so I had no way of knowing how recent it had happened. The wind was blowing constantly, making it impossible to find footprints in the snow. But something deep in my gut told me that trouble was on the way.

Julie curled up on the couch next to Daisy, worry etched deep on her face as she pressed a cold washcloth to Daisy's forehead.

"I don't feel good, mama," Daisy said, the sadness in her voice breaking my heart.

"I know, sweetheart. I'm so sorry you're not feeling well."

"What does she need?" I asked, pacing behind the couch because I felt helpless.

"We're doing everything we can right now," Julie replied

with a heavy sigh. "I'm trying to get her to drink fluids and giving her Tylenol for the fever. My mom is making chicken noodle soup. Unfortunately, this is just something that will have to pass. Hopefully it does quickly."

"Do you want me to run to the store and grab anything?" I offered as I felt Patrick's hand clasp my shoulder. I looked at him, confused because it wasn't like we were friends.

"No. Thank you, though. It's very sweet of you to offer."

I nodded and then glanced at Patrick, wondering what he was up to.

"Come help me with the lights outside," he said.

I arched an eyebrow but didn't want to worry Julie as she returned her worried focus to Daisy. I grabbed my jacket from the coat rack and stepped outside with him, pulling the door closed behind me.

"What's up?" I asked, shivering as a gust of cold air rushed between us.

"I just got a call from my friend, Keith, in Colorado. He has ways of tracking people, and after I told him what was going on, he put a trace on Joel's cell phone. Turns out that he's here—in Silver Falls. He checked into a motel two days ago."

"Are you fucking kidding me?" I shoved a hand through my hair and looked around, as if he would magically appear.

"I wish I were, but honestly, I expected it."

"How so?"

"The asshole is clearly obsessed with Julie and went as far as hiding an AirTag in Daisy's toy. We all knew he would figure out where they were sooner or later. At least we know that he's here, so he can't surprise us."

"What do we do now?"

Patrick shrugged and let out a deep breath as he looked around, surveying the deep woods around us.

"Now we stay alert and wait for him to make his move."

<u>Twenty</u>

Julie

"You need to eat, dear," my mother said as she gently squeezed my shoulder from over the back of the couch.

"I'm not hungry."

I hadn't eaten all day because Daisy seemed to be getting worse instead of better, and I was trying my best not to worry. We were far enough from the city that the thought of her needing to be rushed to the hospital made me uneasy as I realized how long it could take us to get there, especially now that it was dark outside and the roads would freeze again.

"I know, but you're not doing her any favors by letting yourself get sick, too. I'll sit with her while you eat. Gage just sat down. Maybe you can join him?"

I didn't miss the hint in her tone, nor did I miss the obvious one with the wink she gave me before walking around and taking a seat at the other end of the couch. Daisy stirred slightly, forcing Duke's head up as he waited to see if she was getting up. She groaned and rolled over, throwing the blanket off of her as a shiver shot through.

"It's okay. I've got her," my mother assured me. "I've taken care of many sick kids, my love. Plus, you'll just be across the room if we need anything."

I pushed a deep breath out through pursed lips and nodded. She was right. It wasn't like I was going anywhere where I couldn't see or hear them. Not only that, but Daisy was still sleeping, which was good because her body needed the rest.

I walked into the kitchen, pausing for a minute when I noticed my father sitting off to the side, his chair beside the window, while he held a bowl of soup in his hands. A baseball bat sat beside him, within reach if he needed it. Patrick was on his phone, his back leaning against the back door, which was never used, but it was almost as if he were blocking it. Then Gage sat at the kitchen table, his face worried, even if he tried to hide it with a smile. I looked around, noticing that he was sitting at the very end of the table, closest to the front door.

"What is going on?" I asked, looking between them with a hand planted firmly on my hip.

I could feel my mother's gaze on me as I glanced over my shoulder to look at her. She always wore her emotions easily, which meant she would give them away if they were hiding something. She quickly looked away from me, pretending to mess with the TV as I returned my focus to the men in the kitchen.

"Someone start talking now," I said, my voice even as an odd calmness washed over me.

"Why don't I fix you a bowl of soup?" Patrick offered as he pushed away from the back door and tucked his phone into his pocket.

"I don't want soup. I want to know what's going on."

He ignored me as he fixed a bowl and then set it down next to Gage, conveniently on the other side of him, where I would be protected. I cocked my head to the side, waiting him out before giving up and staring at Gage. He shifted nervously in his chair as he lifted the spoon to his lips and took a sip of the broth. I looked down into his bowl, noticing that was all that was left.

Gage was a quick eater, and while I would love to think that he was purposely going slow so he could eat with me, I knew better. If that were what he was doing, he would have waited for me before he started eating. Instead, he had already eaten and was pretending to be finishing up so he could sit there and do whatever it was he was doing.

I inhaled sharply through my nose and blew it out, trying not to allow myself to get too upset. I was tired and cranky from not eating all day, all while the stress of Daisy being sick had started to pile up on me.

Just then, my phone dinged with a new text message, followed quickly by another as more messages arrived. I pulled out my phone and opened the messages, noticing they all came from an unknown number. My heart hammered in my chest as I read them, right as the power went out. The screen on my phone lit up the space around me as a chill snaked down my back.

Unknown: Did you really think I wouldn't find you?

Unknown: There's nowhere left to go, Julie.

Unknown: But since you like to play games, how about we play one of my favorites?

Unknown: You try to hide, and I'll hunt you.

Unknown: Ready?

Unknown: Hopefully, I don't mistake one of your family members as a threat. I would really hate for anything bad to happen to them, like it did to your husband.

Twenty-One
Gage

"Son of a bitch!" Julie growled, her tone a mix of anger and fear as the power went out, casting us into darkness. I was at her side within a matter of seconds, my hand protectively wrapped around her waist while Patrick and her father talked quickly. Flashlights on phones were turned on while I focused on Julie, her body rigid and trembling beneath my touch.

"Hey, are you okay?" I asked. "What happened?"

"Yeah," she whispered, her body trembling beneath my touch. "I got a handful of text messages from an unknown number. I mean, it's unknown, but it's also very clearly Joel."

"What did they say?"

"Which one? He sent several, each of them equally disturbing," she said, her voice wary as she turned her phone toward me so I could read them.

I pressed my lips together to keep from saying something stupid since Patrick hadn't told her the full extent of what was happening. Just then, Duke got up from beside the couch and began growling a low, deep growl.

"Go sit with Mom," Patrick said, guiding his dad out of the way as he rushed past us, pulling the curtain back and checking the front porch even though it was pitch black outside. "I don't fucking like this one bit. I can't see shit outside."

"The generator should have kicked on by now," I muttered, realizing quickly that it hadn't. "Fuck."

I glanced at Julie, hating how terrified she looked.

"Let's get you to the couch," I said, guiding her there quickly, making sure not to trip over Duke as he continued growling at the front door while he stood next to Daisy, who stayed asleep on the couch. "Duke, go check."

He immediately went to the front door and stood there, staring at it with an intensity that sent a chill through me. While he was calm most of the time, Duke had been trained as a protection dog from a very early age by one of the best trainers I had ever met. I didn't realize until now how handy his training would be. Once Julie was sitting on the couch with Daisy between her and her mother, I walked over to where Duke was standing in front of the door, his posture rigid and ready to attack.

"Should we open it and let him out?" Patrick asked, staring at my dog.

"We could, but I worry about us not being able to see much out there. I would rather keep him in here while the threat is contained outside. But I think this answers the question about when the lock was cut off the shed."

"Yep. It would also explain the power tool noise Mom heard last night," Patrick noted. "The wind must have blown away his tracks. That's why we didn't see anything this morning."

I nodded, completely oblivious to anyone else in the room for a moment while my mind raced, putting the pieces together.

"Umm… Threat?" Julie questioned, turning to look at us. "What threat?"

"I think it's time to tell her," I said quietly to Patrick, taking a step back as he nodded.

"Tell me what?" Her tone was sharp as her eyes narrowed on her brother.

"We found some stuff at your apartment," Patrick said with a heavy sigh.

"Stuff? What kind of stuff?"

"Adoption papers for one. Family photos that had Joel's head glued over Mike's. The worst is that he had…" Patrick tipped his head back and shook it, not wanting to say the words as his throat tightened with emotion.

"He had what?" Julie asked, looking between him and her parents. "Just tell me. Whatever it is, I can handle it."

Lynn leaned forward and squeezed Julie's hand before speaking.

"He left the keychain that you'd given Mike for Christmas on the kitchen table with the photos. On the back of it, he crossed out Mike's name and carved in the words: You were mine first."

Julie gasped loudly and covered her face with her hand as the tears streaked her cheeks.

"I thought it was lost—" she sobbed. "How did he get it?"

"We don't know," her mother assured her. "But the point is that he had it, and he's made his interest in you very clear. We didn't want to tell you and stress you out with everything else that's been going on."

"You should have told me," Julie fumed, turning her anger to Patrick while Duke continued staring at the front door and letting out low growls.

There was no point in letting him continue if I wasn't going to let him outside, so I went over, grabbed a few treats from the container, and slipped one to him after asking him to come. He went right back to Daisy's side and sat beside her as he ate them.

"I didn't want to upset you," Patrick repeated with another heavy sigh.

"That's not the point!" Julie said harshly, throwing her hands in the air. "You can't keep information like that from me. This guy is dangerous. I deserve to know everything, so please stop keeping things from me and just tell me the truth."

"You want to know the truth?" Patrick asked, leaning over the couch and staring at her. She nodded but didn't say anything. "The truth is that I have a friend who's been tracing his cell phone, and guess what? He's here in town and has been for a few days. So, yeah, Julie, excuse me for keeping things to myself while I rush to figure out how to keep you safe from this asshole. No matter what we do, he's constantly five steps ahead of us."

"He's here?" she whispered, her eyes wide with fear again.

Patrick nodded.

"Well, his messages make more sense now," Julie said sadly.

"What did they say?" Patrick asked.

"Long story short, that he found me and that he wanted to play a game where I hide and he tries to hunt me. Then he mentioned something about not wanting to mistake any of you for intruders because he didn't want anything bad to happen to my family like it did to Mike."

I clenched my fists at my side, hating how helpless I felt.

"What's the plan? What do we do now?" I asked, looking at Patrick and hoping he had one.

"I think the best thing for now is to find a safe room and all of us stay in there until morning. It's obvious that he cut the power as a whole, so we can't rely on the generator. I don't like being unprepared, but I would feel better if we were all together. We'll call the police and see if they can send someone out to check things. With the storm, who knows how long that will take." Patrick's jaw clenched as he spoke, his fists balled at his sides.

"I'm calling the police now," Dave, Julie's father, said, holding his phone to his ear. "I'll let them know what's going on and make sure they have it on record that there's a possible intruder on the property. Silver Falls Police Department doesn't take kindly to this kind of stuff, so I'm sure they'll send someone out as quickly as they can."

"We can go to the room we stayed in last night," Lynn offered. "It only has one window, but a joining bathroom and three beds. You guys can take turns sleeping while someone watches the house."

"That works for me," I said, agreeing with her. "What do you need for Daisy? I want to make sure that we take everything we might need with us in there so we don't have to come out for anything until the morning."

"Tylenol and some Gatorade. Maybe some packs of crackers or other snack food if she wakes up hungry. I'll take extra clothes in there in case she needs to change. Mom, can you gather extra bedding? It's going to be cold without the heater," Julie said, her mind working as quickly as mine as she realized the gravity of our situation.

"I'm on it," Lynn said, getting up and accepting the hand her husband offered before they went together to gather supplies.

"There's only one easy way inside right now, so I'll stay guarding this door while you guys gather everything you need. We'll hear if he tries to come through the back door since it sticks, or if he breaks any windows. I can't imagine he'll attempt trying to come in through an upstairs window, but who knows with this guy. I trust that he's not already inside the house, or else the dog would be going crazy," Patrick said to me and Julie. "Though I do wish I had a weapon on me."

"I'll let Julie get what she needs while I go grab my grandmother's shotgun," I offered, noticing the way Patrick's eyebrows lifted.

"Your grandmother had a shotgun?" he asked as a smile tugged at the corners of his lips.

"She did. I bought it for her right after my grandfather

passed away, and she insisted on staying up here by herself. I took her out shooting one day to make sure she was comfortable using it. Let's just say that we didn't have to practice too long, and I could hear my grandfather laughing from heaven when she took down every single tin can that I had set up for her without even trying."

"Go, Granny," Julie said with a warm smile. "I want to be her when I grow up."

I smiled back at her and let out the first relaxed breath I'd had all night. She went and gathered the things she needed while I made myself useful and got the rest. It would be weird sharing a room with everyone tonight, but I loved that we were all on the same page with keeping Julie and Daisy safe. While my grandmother wasn't here to put a bullet in Joel's head, I had no problem stepping in and doing it in her honor.

Twenty-Two

Julie

The bedroom was cold, despite the body heat of six people and a dog. I sat on the bed, shivering under the blankets as Daisy curled up next to me. Her fever had broken a few hours ago, and I was thankful that she seemed to be feeling a little better when she got up to use the bathroom.

Patrick and my dad were sleeping, while my mother, Gage, and I stayed awake. It was hard not to be on edge, but every time I looked at Gage, I felt an overwhelming sense of calmness wash over me. Even knowing that his grandmother's shotgun and ammunition were stored just a few feet away in the closet, I didn't feel like I needed it to feel safe because Gage created that feeling for me on his own.

My mother shifted on the bed her and my father were sharing. It was small and cramped, but they managed to make it work. We had tried to bring in a few chairs since the beds weren't too big, but the room quickly became crowded. There had only been enough room for one, which was where Gage sat with Duke at his feet. A few candles provided soft light, allowing us to be aware of our surroundings without being too much, so that the others could sleep.

It was after three in the morning, and I was restless, my body aching as I struggled to find a comfortable position.

"Do you want to sit here?" Gage offered, already getting up before I could stop him.

"No, but thank you. I'm okay here."

"No, you're not. Come sit in the chair, and I'll go sit with Daisy."

"It's fine. Really. Thank you, though."

Before I could continue to object, Gage was standing in front of me, watching me as he held his hand out to help me up. I sighed heavily, too tired to fight with him. As soon as I stood up, Daisy rolled over, taking up the entire bed as she spread out and started snoring loudly.

I covered my mouth with my hands to keep from laughing as we watched her. His shoulders shook slightly as he chuckled, his face so handsome with the giant smile that spread across it. He loved my daughter, that was for sure. I couldn't imagine any other man, besides my dad and brother, who would allow my daughter to paint their fingernails pink and not complain about it. But Gage hadn't just let her paint his nails; he bragged about them and made sure to show everyone what a great job she did, which only made my heart love him more than it was supposed to.

"Go sit in the chair and I'll sit on the floor," he said, pressing his hand to my lower back and moving me out of the way before he plopped down.

I hated that he was going to be just as uncomfortable on the floor, so I pushed the chair out of the way and sat down with him. The bed had been pushed against the wall, creating a safe space for Daisy to sleep. I sat on the side facing my mother, who was now resting with her eyes closed, trying to stay upright beside my dad.

"Mom, you should get some sleep. Gage and I can handle things and wake you up if we need anything."

Her eyes opened slowly as she gave me a soft smile.

"I'm sorry, dear. I hadn't realized how tired I was. I'm going to use the restroom, and then I think I'll take you up on that offer."

She turned and put her feet on the hardwood floor, accidentally kicking something out from underneath the bed. I reached over and grabbed it, making sure she didn't trip over it. My eyebrows furrowed as I held the manila folder in my hand and slowly opened it.

My mother let out a soft gasp as I quickly flipped through the pages, staring in horror at the adoption paperwork that had already been completed and signed by Joel. The only thing missing was my signature.

"Why do you have this?" I asked, looking up at her with mixed horror and rage.

She opened her mouth to say something, but closed it instead, offering a small shrug.

"Mom, you guys should have left this at the apartment. This could be evidence. Now it has all of our fingerprints on it, so who knows if it still has his? How are the police going to lock him up if the incriminating evidence is missing?"

"There was never a plan to show it to the police," Patrick said, clearing his voice as he sighed heavily and kept his eyes closed as he laid on the bed.

"Aren't you supposed to be sleeping?"

"I'm resting, Julie. That's as good as it's going to get right now."

"You're so stubborn," I grumbled, looking through the rest of the papers. My fingers trembled as I saw the stack of photos where Joel had glued his head where Mike's had been. Even in the dim light, the sight was enough to make my blood curdle.

"Wait—what do you mean there was never a plan to show this to the police?" I asked, setting the papers down in my lap as I turned my head and stared at my brother once his words finally caught up to me.

He sighed heavily, turning his head to look at me.

"I have no intention of going to the police with any of this," he clarified.

"What?" My eyes nearly bulged out of my head. "Why not?"

"Because what I plan to do to him doesn't involve the cops. In fact, it's better that they don't know anything to begin with."

"Then why did you have Dad call the police earlier if you don't want them involved?"

"There's a trail for everything. If it shows that we called the cops as soon as we felt there was a threat up here, then we have more on our side to show it's justified if we accidentally shoot and kill an armed intruder. That is, if the cops show up before I can dispose of the body. It's just a little added protection in case we need it."

"You can't be serious," I stammered, my mind struggling to process everything he was saying as Gage's hand rested lightly on my thigh.

"I told you—I don't fuck around when it comes to my family, Julie."

Twenty-Three
Gage

"You need to sleep," Patrick scolded as he stood at the foot of the bed and stared down at where his sister was asleep on my shoulder.

I didn't know what time she finally fell asleep, but I was thankful that she was resting. It had been a long day, followed by an even longer night, and I didn't want her to catch whatever cold Daisy had. The sun had already come up, and her parents had taken Daisy into the living room after Patrick and Dave made sure everything was safe. Duke had been calm for once, which made me feel more at ease that whatever threat there had been was gone. On top of everything, the power had come back on sometime early this morning, which made me question whether it had anything to do with Joel. While Duke had been on alert last night, there were also strong winds that wreaked havoc outside, which may have triggered him.

"I'm fine," I lied, trying not to move so I didn't wake Julie.

"You're a shitty liar. I'll take her to her room. Which one is it?"

"They've been sleeping in the room next to mine. Other hall, down at the very end," I answered, knowing he wasn't going to give up.

He bent down and reached for Julie right as her eyes fluttered open and she jolted beside me.

"What's wrong?" she asked, looking around panicked. "Where's Daisy?"

"Everything is fine," Patrick assured her as he squatted in front of her. "Daisy is in the living room with Mom and Dad. They got up about an hour ago. She's been fever-free and has an appetite, so Dad is making her French toast while Mom sits with her on the couch."

"Is that safe?" Julie questioned, looking from her brother to me.

"Duke is with them," I assured her. "Patrick and your dad checked the house before they took Daisy out there."

"You need to get some sleep," Patrick told her, his eyes showing the lack of sleep he had gotten.

"You're one to talk," she argued.

"Yeah, but I don't have a daughter who needs me to take care of her. We've got Daisy for a bit. Try to get a few hours of sleep in while you can."

Patrick stood up and gave me a nod before walking out of the bedroom and pulling the door closed behind him.

"Want me to help you up?" I offered as I stood and extended my hand to her.

"I can't remember the last time I was this tired," she

replied, taking it. "I don't even care where I sleep. I just want to pass out for a few hours."

Before I could object, she crawled into the bed Daisy had slept in, pulled the blanket up around her, and was out. I wasn't about to leave her by herself, so I picked one of the other beds, grabbed a blanket, and followed suit.

****

I had no idea how much time had passed once I finally woke up, but when my eyes opened, my heart sank when I noticed Julie was gone. I got up and made my way to the living room, where Patrick and her dad were watching TV while Julie and her mom sat with Daisy at the kitchen table.

Daisy looked like she was feeling better, but it was the worried look on Julie's face that had the hairs on my arms standing up. I hated that, thanks to that asshole, Joel, we were all constantly on guard.

I frowned as I walked over to the coffee maker and tried to figure out what was going on as I made myself a strong cup.

"There's still plenty of time to send your letter in, honey," Lynn said softly as she gently rested her hand on Daisy's arm. "Why don't we put a few things on it and then your granddad and I can make a trip into town to drop it off?"

"But what if he doesn't get it? Santa doesn't even know that we're not home. What if he takes presents to the apartment and is mad because we aren't there?" Daisy asked, her lower lip trembling.

I let my head fall back on my neck when I realized what was happening.

"Santa knows a lot, my love," Julie assured her. "Trust me, he will find you wherever you are. He won't forget about you this Christmas. I promise you that won't happen."

"But I don't even want anything. I just… I just… I want to go home!" Daisy cried out, throwing her hands on the table as she erupted in tears.

Julie covered her mouth with her hands as she tried to fight the tears before reaching for her daughter. She leaned over and turned the chair so she could reach Daisy before scooping her up and pulling her onto her lap, where she held her.

"Honey, what's wrong?" Julie asked, rocking slowly as she kept her arms locked around her daughter. "Do you not like it up here?"

"It's not that," Daisy replied with a sob. "Last year, we did a lot for Christmas, and it was fun. This year, we haven't shopped for presents, and you seem really sad. I miss how Christmas used to be when we lived in the apartment. It was the best."

Julie closed her eyes and rested her head against Daisy's.

"Guess what I heard on the news this morning?" I said, standing in front of them as I noticed the worried creases in Julie's forehead.

"What?" Daisy asked, looking up at me with the most beautiful eyes I'd ever seen.

"I heard that they got the roads cleared, so we can head into town. I thought we could visit some stores and do some Christmas shopping if you'd like. Thanks to that blizzard, I haven't had a chance to get anything for anyone yet, and it's left me feeling a little frazzled myself." I made a silly face, hoping it would drive the point home.

"What's frazzled mean?"

"It's kind of like, silly," Julie answered for her. "And I think that's a fantastic idea, because I've been feeling a little frazzled myself."

"Well, then, I guess there's only one thing left to do," I said, wiggling my eyebrows and pressing my palms together as I pretended to be working out some evil plan. "Let's go shopping!"

"Yay!" Daisy cheered, climbing off her mother's lap to give me a high five.

I knew that we were all worried about when and where Joel would appear, but I wasn't going to put Christmas on hold and ruin a child's holiday just because some asshole was obsessed with the woman I loved.

134

<u>Twenty-Four</u>
Julie

My palms were sweaty despite the below-freezing temperatures outside. Even though the roads had been cleared, that didn't mean that the weather had improved. Snow blew around us, dusting the freshly cleared streets as we made our way down Main Street.

It had been years since I'd been to Silver Falls, and I'd forgotten just how charming the small town was at Christmas. The street was lit up with strings of soft white Christmas lights and pretty red bows tied to the light posts. All the shops were busy with people bustling about, trying to finish their Christmas shopping. I knew how much Daisy would love going into each of the shops because they all felt so magical, but we were headed to the one store that could top all of that: Silver Falls Express.

Silver Falls Express had everything a child could ever dream of, from toys galore to Santa's workshop, where they could watch the elves make toys. There was also an area in the back of the store where children could visit Santa and take pictures with him. I'd brought the letter Daisy had written so we could drop it off at the North Pole. I figured it was the best way to bring back some of the holiday cheer and ignite the Christmas magic she so desperately needed.

We pulled up outside, and her eyes widened in shock as she stared at the gigantic store in front of us.

"What is that?" she asked, leaning forward to try to see it better.

Patrick and Gage laughed as they unbuckled and climbed out of Patrick's beast of a truck. My parents had decided to stay at the inn and work on a few things there—though they wouldn't tell me what. We figured Patrick's truck would be the best to get us through any bad weather—or to run someone over with, as he put it.

I helped Daisy out of her booster seat and watched as Patrick smiled as she wrapped her arms around his neck and refused to let him set her down. I laughed and took Gage's hand as he assisted me so I didn't fall on my ass trying to get out of the truck. Between the lift and the black ice that lurked beneath the thin blanket of snow, I had a lot counting against me getting out successfully on my own.

We walked into the store, and I grinned when I saw Daisy's eyes light up. The store was packed, which I expected, but I couldn't stop the panicked feeling that kept threatening to consume me as I realized just how many people were there. Not only was it easy for a child to get lost in a place like this, but it was also incredibly easy for someone to blend in with the crowd and watch us without our noticing.

"Everything will be fine," Gage assured me, pulling me into his side as his fingers gently dug into my hip. "We've got eyes on everyone. You just need to focus on shopping with Daisy."

I nodded, forcing a smile as I tried not to let my worry ruin the day for her.

"Okay, my love, where should we start?" I asked, pulling her to the side so we were out of the way as I bent down and smiled at her. "Do we want to shop for toys first? Or should we go say hi to Santa real quick?"

"Santa is here?" she questioned in disbelief, her eyes widening.

"He is. Do you want to go say hi and take your picture with him?"

She nodded quickly as she reached for my hand and let me lead the way.

I didn't have to look behind me to know that Patrick and Gage were right there, keeping a close watch on everyone and everything. The line for Santa was surprisingly short, which was comforting. I glanced down at Daisy, loving the way her little face lit up as she took everything in. From the elves rushing around to the soft Christmas music playing overhead to the stage right before us where Santa and Mrs. Claus sat, everything was beautiful and perfect.

"Santa is ready to see you," a cheery elf said, extending her hand to invite Daisy to go see him. Daisy looked nervously at me, then over her shoulder at the guys.

"Can they come with us?" she asked.

"Of course," the elf replied. "Why don't we get you settled on Santa's chair so you can tell him what you want for Christmas, then we'll get a picture with everyone?"

"Yes, please!" Daisy said, beaming.

I scrunched my face in apology at the guys before following Daisy's lead over to Santa and Mrs. Claus. The elf helped Daisy climb up onto the large, wooden arm of Santa's chair so she wasn't sitting on his lap but was close enough to tell him what she wanted for Christmas. I tried to lean forward so I could hear too, but she lowered her voice and spoke behind her hand to keep us from hearing.

Patrick and Gage exchanged a confused look with me, none of us knowing what that was all about. Santa's eyebrows rose as he looked at us and then nodded his head before whispering something back to her. Daisy turned to face us, a huge grin spread across her face that I hadn't seen in a while.

"Are we ready for our photo?" the elf asked.

Santa nodded as Mrs. Claus reached behind Daisy to hold his hand as she sat between them.

"Perfect! We'll get one shot with the three of you, and then we'll add the adults in," the elf said as they stood at the camera mounted to the tripod and started pressing buttons. "Smile!"

Daisy continued to smile and hold still while the elf got a few pictures before waving for us to join them.

"Alright, if we can have Mom in the middle with each of you on one side of her, please," the elf continued, looking at us as she pointed where she wanted us to go.

We all got lined up, and I couldn't help the flutter that rushed through my chest the second Gage's fingers brushed against mine. I smiled a real, genuine smile that had nothing to do with the holiday photo we were taking and everything to do with him.

"You guys did great! We will have these ready in a few minutes if you want to stop by the workshop to view them." The elf smiled and gave us a wave as we walked off the stage and exited into the calmer part of the store.

"That was so much fun!" Daisy squealed, squeezing my hand. "Can we buy the pictures? Please!"

"Oh. Umm…" I didn't know how to respond to that because I knew how expensive these things could be, and I didn't have the luxury of overspending right now when I didn't have a job.

"I'll buy the photos and meet you guys in the toys," Patrick said, not giving me an option to disagree as he winked at Daisy and walked off.

"Okay," I replied through gritted teeth as I narrowed my eyes at my brother, trying to keep my irritation to a minimum. I knew he meant well, but I didn't need him teaching Daisy that she could have everything she wanted. I turned to Daisy and smiled. "Shall we go do some shopping?"

Daisy let out another squeal and pulled on my hand as she dragged me through the crowd and back to the toy section we had passed by earlier.

<u>Twenty-Five</u>
Joel

I stood off to the side, watching as Julie and Daisy looked at toys. I'd been following them for over thirty minutes, and she hadn't noticed me yet, which was the whole plan. I knew that I would have to get them away from the two assholes they'd come with. All I had to do was separate Daisy from Julie, and the rest would be easy.

Julie looked tired as she tried to hide a yawn while smiling as Daisy picked up a doll and showed it to her. Julie smiled and nodded her head, but I could see how exhausted she was. It was probably because they were freaked out last night after I cut the power. Daisy had left Uni in the bedroom with her, so I had been able to watch the entire show they put on with everyone hiding in the same room, waiting for me to make a move.

The problem was, I wasn't stupid.

I knew that the second I tried to step into that house, her brother or the asshole she was sleeping with would attack me.

I didn't care about anyone other than Julie, and nothing would stand in my way of having her.

<u>Twenty-Six</u>

Julie

"Are you sure that's the one you want?" I asked, looking at Daisy as her eyes watered.

She nodded, trying not to let her emotions show as we stared at the box she was holding, which held a baby doll with dark brown hair and freckles lightly splattered across her nose. It was the last one they had, and someone had torn open the box and stolen the accessories that went with it.

"I'll go up to the front and see if they can check in the back," Patrick offered, smiling at Daisy.

"Thank you. I appreciate it," I said, sighing when I looked at the shopping cart that was nearly overflowing with toys Daisy had already picked out.

The goal was to make a list of what she really wanted, and then we would put the items back so she could be surprised on Christmas Day. Or at least, that was my plan. Apparently, Gage and my brother had plans of their own and were going to buy it all when I took Daisy back to the truck in a bit so we could head to another store. Thankfully, Patrick had a cover over the bed of his truck so he could stash everything without her seeing.

"I can't tell which dolls they are, but I can see some boxes up there," Gage said, nodding to the very top of the shelf. "If I pick you up, can you check them?"

"You want to pick me up?"

"Yeah. If I try to climb the shelf, I'll pull the entire thing down. If I pick you up, you can quickly check whether any of them is the one we're looking for. It will be quick and easy."

I glanced at Daisy, hating the hopeful look on her little face.

"Okay. Yeah. Let's check it out," I said, smiling at her before turning to Gage.

"Turn around, and I will pick you up from behind."

I did as he asked and tried to ignore the heat that flushed through my body once his hands touched it. He was incredibly strong as he hoisted me in the air, lifting me high enough to see the top of the shelf. I quickly reached forward and started going through the boxes, setting them aside in a new pile as I started to lose hope.

"Can you move to the right?" I asked, looking down to make sure Daisy was okay. She smiled up at me, seeming delighted that we were doing this for her.

Gage moved a few steps to the right, and I began sorting through those boxes. There was far more to go through in this stack than there had been in the other. I had almost given up hope when I picked up the last box and squealed.

"Oh my God! I found it!" I exclaimed, a wide grin taking over my face as Gage lowered me back to the floor.

I spun around to show Daisy, and my heart dropped when I realized she wasn't there. Sitting on the floor where she had stood was the box she had been holding with the doll inside.

Gage's smile immediately vanished as he looked around and couldn't find her either.

"Daisy!" I screamed, dropping the box as I took off running frantically.

Twenty-Seven
Gage

My heart hammered in my chest as I stared in disbelief at the space Daisy had stood just a few minutes ago. How had she just vanished into thin air?

Julie took off running, frantically screaming Daisy's name while I went in the opposite direction. I ran through the aisles, leaning up on my tiptoes to see over as many heads as I could while I tried to find her. The blood pulsed in my ears as I pushed my way through the crowded space, shouting her name as loudly as I could.

Patrick was walking down the main aisle when he spotted me and came to a stop. I shook my head, my jaw tight as I clenched it and tried to stay calm. I couldn't afford to lose my shit right now because I needed to stay clear-headed so we could find Daisy.

"What the fuck happened?" he growled, standing inches away from me.

"She's gone," I answered tightly, shoving a hand through my hair as I watched his features change. His face hardened as he took off running to the front of the store.

"Daisy!" I called out loudly, repeating her name over and over as I rushed through the store.

"Hey, watch out," a woman snapped as I bumped into her.

"I'm sorry. Have you seen a little girl? She's about this tall and has long dark brown hair and green eyes," I said quickly, praying for someone to help us find her.

"No. But there are kids everywhere, so it's hard to tell. What is she wearing?"

My mind raced as I struggled to remember. Why hadn't I thought of that? There were easily over a hundred kids in the store, many who would fit her description.

"Ummm. She had on a red sweater with a heart on it, I think?"

"I'm sorry. It doesn't ring a bell. I'll keep an eye out for her, though," the woman answered before returning her focus to the toys on the shelf beside her.

I took off sprinting through the store again, stopping as I heard the crackling overhead before the Christmas music was replaced with an announcement.

"Attention all employees, we have a Code Adam. Repeat, we have a Code Adam. Little girl, age five, with brown hair and green eyes. Last seen wearing a red sweater and black pants."

The speaker stopped as people started whispering around me. I didn't have time to stop and listen because Daisy was still missing. I took off down the aisles, calling her name as loudly as I could, praying she would hear me.

Twenty-Eight
Julie

"Where was the last place you saw her?" a male cop asked as I sat in the uncomfortable chair in the security office and continued answering questions.

"She was right beside me on the toy aisle. We were trying to find a doll that she wanted. My friend lifted me so I could look through the boxes on top of the shelf. I checked on her once, and she was still there."

"How long would you say you were distracted with finding the doll?"

"I wasn't—" I started, but then stopped, the realization crashing over me.

I had been distracted with finding the doll because it had meant so much to her that I wanted nothing more than her happiness. I had allowed myself to focus on that instead of keeping our guard up. If we had wraited and asked an employee to look for us instead, Daisy would never have gone missing.

"It wasn't more than a few minutes at most," I sobbed, shaking my head.

"Unfortunately, things like this can happen within seconds. Is there any part of the store that Daisy might have wandered off to? Maybe there was another toy that she had seen and wanted to check out again?"

"No. She wouldn't do that. Daisy isn't the kind of kid who goes wandering."

"Did you see anyone come down the aisle you were on that might have—"

"I think I found something," the young kid who worked at Silver Falls Express said, pointing to one of the monitors.

We all leaned in and watched as he pressed play, showing us on the aisle as Gage lifted me. In the video, I turn to say something, and then I look at Daisy before Gage takes a step to the right, and I start sorting through those boxes. Just then, Daisy looks to the left and then sets the box down before walking down the aisle and disappearing around the corner.

"Is there more? Does it show where she went?" I asked, gripping the arms of the chair so tightly my fingers hurt.

"Let me switch to that camera view real quick," he said, noting the time stamp on the current screen before clicking on another screen and rewinding the video until it matched the time stamp.

I held my breath as I watched someone stand at the end of the aisle wearing a hoodie that covered their face. They waved to her, calling her to them before she walked off. I shook my head in disbelief. While I knew that she was gone, seeing the concrete proof of it was soul-shattering.

"Do you know anyone she would willingly go to like that?" the female officer asked right as the door opened and Patrick stepped in, his face red from the cold and rigid with anger.

"You need to see this," he said, shaking his head. "I went out to the truck to make sure she didn't somehow go out there when we weren't looking, and I found this tucked into the door handle."

He held the note out to the female officer, who tilted her head as she read it out loud. Everything would be considered evidence at this point, so it was best that no one else touched it until it could be secured to preserve fingerprints.

"I warned you not to leave. Now look what you've done." She pulled her head back and glanced at the male officer, who discreetly turned to the side and talked into the two-way radio attached to his shoulder. "Do you know who might have left this note?"

I nodded, looking at Patrick before looking back to her. I knew he didn't want to involve the cops, but it was too late for that. My daughter was missing and in the hands of a madman, which meant I would do anything in my power to get her back.

"My boss, Joel Roberts. He took my daughter."

Twenty-Nine
Joel

"Do you like it?" I asked Daisy as she sat in the seat beside me and stared at the toy I had given her while I drove, trying to get away from Silver Falls Express as quickly as possible. I knew it was only a matter of time before they reported Daisy as missing. Once they did, the entire store would shut down as employees worked quickly to locate her. Thankfully, we were already in the car before that could happen, but the last thing I needed was someone reporting a suspicious person leaving with a child who matched the description.

"Yeah. But when do I get to see Mommy?"

"In a little bit. I told you, we don't want to ruin the surprise for her. She's going to be so happy when she sees you."

"I'm not supposed to leave her side when we're at the store. Can you please take me back? I don't want to get in trouble."

"Trust me, everything will be just fine. You'll see."

I had told her I had a gift for Julie in my car and asked if she could help me surprise her mom. I knew that Daisy would do anything for her mom, so it was easy to convince her to leave the store. Getting her in the car was another story, but thankfully, I made up an excuse about needing to wrap the gift and how it was too cold to do it outside.

I turned the music up so she couldn't keep talking as I made my way through the wooded area and watched the snow fall. It was a long drive, but worth the extra effort to be as far away from people as possible. Not only that, it was closer to where Julie had been staying, which made it easier to keep an eye on her.

An hour later, the cabin that Julie had been staying at came into view. I noticed Daisy's excitement as she saw it when I glanced at her.

But before she could say anything, I grabbed the pill from the middle console and turned toward her as I stopped the car.

"Open your mouth," I commanded, my tone harsher than I intended.

Her eyes widened as she stared at me, confused.

"Now, Daisy. Open your mouth."

Her lower lip trembled as she did as I asked.

"Lift your tongue."

She shook her head, tears welling up in her eyes.

"NOW!" I shouted, making her flinch in the seat beside me.

Her whole body shook as she lifted her tongue and watched in horror as I set the tablet of Phenergan under it.

I had debated on giving her two, but the pharmacist I spoke to confirmed that one was the appropriate dosage for a child. I had faked a stomach bug and did a video visit to get the prescription, claiming that it was the only medication that worked for me after doing plenty of research on its effectiveness in knocking children out. When I went to pick it up, I told them that there would be another prescription coming in soon for my child, but in the meantime, I planned to share mine since we were both so sick. I was honestly surprised at how easily they gave me the information without scolding me about the importance of not sharing a prescription.

A few minutes went by as she sat there calmly staring out the window. She was such a good kid and didn't give me any trouble, which reassured me that she would continue to be trouble-free once I became her new dad. While I knew Julie's brother had taken the copy of the adoption paperwork I left for them at Julie's apartment, I still had the other copy with me. All I needed was Julie's signature, and I could get it filed.

Her body relaxed more, sagging further down in the seat as the drug took its effect. I grinned and started driving now that I knew she wouldn't be able to clearly identify where we were. I drove past the cabin they were staying in and worked my way through the thick forest until I reached the two abandoned cabins. One was close enough to Julie's place that you could see it from the front porch. The other was tucked even further away, where no one would ever think to look.

Thirty
Julie

I was numb. Absolutely, completely numb as I sat at the kitchen table while everyone talked around me.

We spent hours with the police, providing them with all the information we had about Joel and any details I could think of to help them locate Daisy. Thankfully, the store printed a second copy of the photo they'd taken of her with Santa and gave it to the police to help locate her. They were also able to use it to assist with the Amber Alert that was sent out, providing an accurate description of what she was wearing. The copy we had purchased was sitting in front of me, reminding me of how my life had changed in the blink of an eye.

We were told to go back to the inn and wait there in case she showed up, but we all knew what it really meant. Each hour that passed made it even less likely that they would find her or Joel. They could be anywhere at this point, and I had no way of knowing if she was okay.

My eyes hurt from crying and my head throbbed from a combination of things.

But none of that mattered.

My daughter was missing, and I only had myself to blame.

Thirty-One
Gage

"Hey," I said softly as I sat in front of Julie and held her hands in mine. "Baby, you need to eat something."

She shook her head and looked away, her eyes reflecting the sadness that filled all of our hearts.

"I know that you don't want to. None of us want to do anything but find Daisy. But you have to take care of yourself. You have to stay strong for Daisy."

"I can't," she said, sniffling as she sucked in a sob. Her face fell as fresh tears trailed down her cheeks. "I can't live without her, Gage. I can't. There's no way I can survive living without my daughter. She's all that I have left. She's my baby."

I leaned forward and pulled her into my arms, placing her on my lap as I wrapped her in a tight hug. Tears slid down my cheeks as I felt my heart break right alongside hers.

"I know, baby. I know. We're going to find her," I assured her, but even I didn't believe the words I said. I wanted to with every fiber of my being, but I also couldn't trust that Joel wouldn't do something stupid, just to hurt Julie.

The living room was filled with the bags of stuff we had bought for Daisy after she went missing. Once they saw the footage of Daisy leaving the store with Joel, the search inside the store was finished, and everyone went about their business. Since we couldn't leave until Julie was finished talking to the police, Patrick and I decided to pay for everything Daisy had picked out, including the baby doll. It wouldn't bring Daisy back, but it at least gave us some inkling of happiness to cling to, knowing that if she came back, she would be so excited to see all of the stuff we bought.

"We're going to go for a walk," Patrick said, standing in front of us. I could tell something was up with him from how he was acting, but I didn't want to question it in front of Julie. She had more than enough to deal with right now.

His eyes lingered on how I was holding her, but I didn't give a fuck. We had far bigger issues right now than me being in love with his sister.

"Can I take Duke with me?" he asked, shoving his hands into his pockets.

"Yeah. That's a great idea. The blanket Daisy's been using is on the couch. Have him sniff it and tell him search. He should be able to use the scent to help look for her."

"Take one of her shirts," Julie said, pulling away slightly to look at her brother. "The one she wore to bed last night is still in the bedroom. I didn't get a chance to put her dirty clothes in the hamper this morning."

"Will do." Patrick leaned down and kissed the top of his sister's head before giving me a nod. "We'll be back in a bit."

I nodded, trying to force a smile at her parents as they waited bundled up by the door while Patrick grabbed Daisy's shirt. He tucked it into the pocket of his hoodie, so Julie didn't have to see it. Once they left, I took a deep breath and looked at her.

"We need to eat," I said again, knowing that I also needed to take care of myself. "There are leftovers in the fridge. Why don't I heat some up?"

Julie nodded, climbing off my lap and wiping her eyes.

I went to the fridge and looked through the options when we heard a ding. I closed the fridge and looked at Julie, who stood at the island, staring at her phone.

Half a second passed before she grabbed it and swiped her fingers along the screen to unlock it. She gasped as her hand covered her mouth, and she stared at the picture.

Joel smiled proudly next to Daisy, who appeared to be sleeping. Her eyes were closed, so it was hard to tell whether she was okay or not. The text came in a few seconds later.

Unknown: Daddy and Daisy's day of fun!

"You fucking psychopath!" she screamed, slamming the phone down onto the counter before she crumbled to the floor, crying harder as I bent down and held her.

"He has my daughter," she cried, clutching my t-shirt in her fists.

"I know, baby. We're going to get her back. I promise. Why don't you call him and see if you can figure out where he is?"

"Should I do that without asking the police first?"

"I don't think they're really going to be able to help with this. They're already searching the town for her. If we tell them that you got another text message from an unknown number, they probably won't be able to track it right away. If you call him, he might be so anxious to talk to you that he tells you where they're at."

"Do you really think that will work?"

"There's only one way to find out."

Thirty-Two

Julie

I stared at the phone as I sat at the kitchen table, trying to get the courage to speak to Joel. It wasn't that I wanted to delay finding my daughter. It was that I had so much anger and hatred toward the man that I wanted to rip his fucking throat out. But if I approached him like that, I knew he wouldn't tell me where Daisy was. Even worse—I worried he would hurt her, just to get back at me.

"Are you ready?" Gage asked, sitting beside me with the phone between us.

I took a deep breath in and exhaled slowly as I nodded. It was now or never. I had to be strong enough to do this because Daisy's life was on the line. I was hoping he would answer the call, since this was the last phone number he had texted from. The other messages had come from a different phone number, so it was clear he was using burner phones.

Gage pressed the call button, and we waited as it rang on speakerphone. My knee bounced nervously beneath the table as we waited through several rings.

"I was wondering when you'd call," Joel said, finally picking up.

"Where is my daughter?" I snarled, my whole body trembling as Gage rested his hand firmly on my knee to make it stop bouncing and to remind me to stay calm. "I want to talk to her." I softened my tone the best I could as I sighed heavily.

"Our little Daisy is currently sleeping. She had quite the busy day."

"I need to know she's okay," I said, trying to hide that I was crying. "Please. Show me that she's okay."

"You'll just have to take my word for it."

"I can't do that. You know how much she means to me. Please, Joel."

"She means a lot to me, too. I thought you knew that by now? There's nothing that I wouldn't do for my family, Julie. I've been taking care of Daisy since she was just a baby. What makes you think I wouldn't take care of her now?"

"She needs her mother. She needs to be with me. Just please tell me where she is and I'll come get her."

"You and I both know that's not how this is going to work. You can't take something that's mine away from me, Julie. I thought I made that clear?"

I covered my mouth as I cried, not knowing what else to say.

"I'll tell you what," he said, his tone changing to the menacing one I heard the night he attacked me. "Instead of me coming to find you, why don't you come find us instead?"

"I don't even know where to begin," I stammered. "Please, just tell me where she is. I promise there won't be any trouble. I just want my daughter."

"Not to worry, we're closer than you think. You come find us, and if you bring anyone with you, I'll put a bullet in your daughter's head. Time is ticking. Tick tock."

Then the line went dead.

166

Thirty-Three

Gage

"This is a terrible fucking idea," I bit out, my body tense as I stared at Julie as she pulled her heavy winter jacket on.

Shortly after the phone call with Joel, Patrick and her parents returned from their walk and reported that it seemed someone was staying at one of the nearby cabins. Duke had gone wild, barking and yanking Patrick's arm to try to get to the cabin, which left us all feeling confident that was where Daisy was. Not only that, but Joel had said they were close, which was helpful. It seemed his interest remained in having Julie and not just in kidnapping her daughter.

"I don't care. Nothing—and I mean nothing is going to keep me from my daughter."

"You don't know what you're walking into. He could hurt you, or worse—kill you."

"If it means keeping Daisy safe, I'm going to do it."

"Julie," I said with a heavy sigh. "I know that you want to save her, but I need you to stop and realize what you're saying. I can't mindlessly sit back and let you go over there knowing there's a good chance you'll get hurt. You and

Daisy mean the world to me, so you can't ask me to do nothing and allow this to happen. I can't stand the thought of what—"

"Gage," she said, interrupting me as she pressed a finger to my lips. "I made a vow when I became a mother that if it ever came down to it and I had to pick between my life or hers, I would choose her. Every. Single. Time. I understand what you're saying, but like I told Patrick, there's nothing any of you can do to stop me. Please stop trying. The longer we spend doing this, the more time I waste getting to Daisy."

"Are you just going to let this happen?" I demanded, turning my anger and attention to Patrick as he leaned against the wall with his foot propped up behind him. "You need to do something. You're her older brother, so act like it!"

He pushed off the wall and walked over to me, wrapping me in an unexpected hug.

"What the fuck are you doing?" I growled, trying to push him off while hating that this might be the very thing that broke me. "Let go of me."

"I know this sucks, but you have to let her do this her way," he said quietly enough that only I could hear. "I love her, too. But we have to let her do this."

He pulled away, and for the first time since we'd had our fight, I saw tears in his eyes.

"So that's it? We just say fuck it and let her walk into danger by herself?" I aggressively wiped a tear as it slid down my cheek, glancing at Julie, who smiled softly at me.

"She can take care of herself," Patrick said, patting his sister's shoulder as he walked past her and down the hall.

Her parents, who had been sitting on the couch, got up and left the room, giving us some privacy. I could see the worry in their eyes and knew they hated this as much as I did. While I wanted to sit down and find another option, deep down, I knew there weren't any.

"I have to do this, Gage. I know you don't like it and that you might not understand, but I have to. I could never live with myself if anything happened to my baby. I've had to live in a world without her father; I refuse to live in one where she doesn't exist."

The tears slid down her cheeks as she tried to wipe them away.

I stalked over to her, closing the distance between us as I pulled her into my arms and hugged her as if my life depended on it. In a way, it did. If something happened to her and she didn't come back, there was no life left for me to live. She may not be able to live in a world without Daisy, but there was no way I could ever live in one without either of them.

"I love you so much, Julie. More than you could ever know," I said as I kissed the top of her head, trying not to break down in front of her.

"I love you, too. I'll be back as soon as I'm able," she replied, the smile trying to hide the lie she'd just said because there was a good chance she wouldn't be back.

I nodded and tilted my head back as I watched her walk out the front door and close it behind her.

Thirty-Four
Julie

The sound of snow crunching beneath my boots was the only thing I could hear besides the wind as blistering cold air whipped past me. I wrapped my arms around myself, trying to stay warm as I trekked through the woods. There appeared to be an undefined path that was already covered in snow, but I followed it because there weren't any other options. There were a few old lamp posts between the cabins that provided a little light, but other than the full moon, it was rather dark. I was thankful that I had enough to guide me so I didn't get lost or trip over something and break my leg before I could get to Daisy.

Soon, I came upon a single cabin, smaller than the inn, but also with a second story. While it looked like it was still in good condition, I didn't trust that they were in it, given how there didn't appear to be any lights on inside. While it was possible that he was forcing her to sit inside with no lights, I couldn't imagine him torturing her like that. Not after seeing all of the photos he'd altered with his face instead of Mike's, and the adoption paperwork. He cared for Daisy, even if it killed me to admit it.

My stomach had been a mess since she'd gone missing, and

I felt this sense of emptiness that I hadn't felt since Mike died. Losing Daisy had been just as gut-wrenching and devastating, but in a way, I felt it deeper than I had when I lost Mike. Maybe it was because she was the only thing I had left of Mike, or maybe it was because she was part of me. I couldn't figure it out, but I knew that I wouldn't feel any ounce of relief until she was with me again.

I continued walking, hating how far I had walked from the inn, but I knew I had to keep going. While I would have loved to have Gage and my brother with me for protection, I wouldn't risk Joel keeping his word and putting a bullet through my daughter's head if I showed up with anyone. He could hurt me however he wanted, but I would do everything I could to keep him from hurting her.

Finally, the trees thinned out, opening to a small clearing with a rundown-looking cabin, where a dim light came from inside.

I pulled in a deep breath as I jogged the short distance over to the door, desperate to see my daughter. My hand trembled as I lifted my fist and banged on the door.

It opened slowly as I looked down and saw Daisy with tears running down her face while a knife was pressed against her throat.

Thirty-Five
Gage

I paced the living room for a solid five minutes before Patrick came out and leaned against the wall, shoving his hands into his pockets.

"You're awfully fucking calm for someone who just sent his sister into danger," I growled, not bothering to hide my frustration and irritation with him.

"Julie is fine," he said without expressing any emotion.

I threw my hands in the air as I stared at him, wondering how he could be so fucking delusional.

"Are you fucking kidding me?"

"No, I'm not fucking kidding you. We have eyes on the cabin. Julie and Daisy are fine."

I stopped pacing and froze where I was.

"What do you mean? Who has eyes on the cabin?"

"My friend Keith, from Colorado. Once he confirmed Joel was in Silver Falls, I filled him in on everything that was happening. He made a call and had his friend, Elizabeth, come down to check things out. While Joel's been sneaking around spying on Julie, she's been doing the same to him. They knew when he checked out of the motel and that he was staying two cabins down from the inn. That's why I went for a walk earlier, to make it look more believable that we just stumbled upon someone being there. As soon as Duke started barking, the lights inside the cabin went off, so he knew we had found him."

"And you're just now telling anyone about this?"

"It wasn't the right time."

"And sending your sister off to some psychopath's cabin was the right time?"

While I was relieved that someone was watching Joel, it didn't make me feel any less concerned about Julie and Daisy being alone in that cabin with him. Just because this person knew he was staying there didn't mean they had eyes inside the cabin, so I wasn't going to rest easy until I knew that both of my girls were safe. I also had no clue who this person was, nor did I trust that they would do anything if the girls were put in immediate danger.

"I couldn't risk telling her about it. If she had known, she would have acted differently when she approached him. He's smart; he would have caught on that something was off. The last thing I want is for him to lose his temper and hurt them. Julie needed to go into this exactly the way she did."

"This feels incredibly reckless," I said, forcing out a harsh breath to try to rein in my frustration.

"I know."

"So what, we just sit here and wait? I don't like being that far from them in case they need help."

"We have no choice. I don't know this woman, Elizabeth, but Keith said to trust her, so I am. It's the best we can do right now."

"I don't like it at all. You can sit there and act like nothing is wrong while Julie puts her life on the line, but I'm not going to."

I grabbed my coat from the hook hanging by the door and shrugged it on as I flung the door open and stalked outside, Duke falling in line right beside me.

"Gage," Patrick called, jogging to keep up with me. "We can't just storm in there. We need to wait until we have an all clear. Elizabeth is keeping Keith updated, and he's going to call me when it's okay for us to go get them."

"Fuck that. Fuck Keith. Fuck Elizabeth. Fuc—"

My words were cut off as a gunshot rang out through the air around us.

Thirty-Six

Julie

"Take one fucking step and the next bullet will go between your eyes," I warned, holding my hands steady as Daisy stood behind me. The small handgun felt oddly comforting in my hands, and I sent up a silent thank you to Gage's grandma for continuing to help me without even knowing it. I had found the gun and some ammunition for it when we first arrived at the inn, while I was putting stuff away for me and Daisy. I hadn't told Gage about it because I had forgotten about it until tonight. I knew I couldn't tell anyone I had it, or they would have tried to talk me out of my plan.

It hadn't taken much for Joel to let me in and put the knife away. But the image of it being held to her throat was enough to make my blood boil, and the rage hadn't stopped bubbling inside me. As soon as I was able to, I pulled her into my arms, hugging her as long as I could before I turned on Joel.

He hadn't bothered to pat me down when I came in, though there hadn't been much time for that. He was so happy to see me that once he saw no one was with me, he closed the door and set the knife down. It was out of my reach, but it didn't matter since I had something more powerful anyway.

"You don't mean that," he said, glancing at the wall where I'd put a bullet through his head in the picture he hung up. It was of Mike and me on our wedding day, but he'd blown it up to poster size and covered Mike's head with a picture of him instead.

"I do mean that. Take one fucking step and it's over."

"After all that I've done for you, this is how you repay me?" he growled, face scrunched as anger washed over it. "I did everything for you. I went out of my way to make sure you had everything you needed after your husband died. I took care of you and Daisy as if you were my family because you were. And this is how you treat me? You stupid, fucking bitch!"

"Don't talk to my mom that way," Daisy said, popping out slightly from behind me with her eyebrows furrowed.

Before I could process what was happening, Joel sprang forward, lunging at Daisy. I put my body in between them, blocking her from him as his body hit me, knocking me to the floor as the gun slid out of my reach.

"Get out of the cabin, Daisy," I said loudly, using the tone that she knew meant I was serious. "NOW!"

She looked at me with terrified eyes as she shook her head. I didn't want her to see what was about to happen. She had already known so much loss at a young age; I wasn't going to ruin her life by letting her watch this monster try to kill me. I vowed to do everything in my power to protect her, and I wasn't going to give up now.

My head and chest hurt from the impact of him falling on me and knocking me to the hard floor. I struggled as I pushed him away, grunting with the effort to lift his weight from my body. His fist collided with my ribs as he punched me repeatedly, creating an immense amount of pain. I exhaled sharply and continued trying to fight him off of me as I brought my knee up, landing a hit right against his groin. He buckled and rolled off of me for a split second as I tried to move away.

I turned and looked at Daisy, hating the horror I saw in her eyes. I didn't have long before he would be on me again, so I had to make it count.

"I'm okay. I need you to go, NOW. Find Gage or Uncle Pat and do not come back to this cabin. Do you understand me?"

She nodded, her lower lip trembling. I wanted to get up, hug her, and tell her everything would be okay, but I couldn't. Before I could get myself up off the floor, I felt Joel's hands on me, pulling me back to him as I held in a scream. I didn't want her to know the fear that I held onto, knowing what he was capable of.

"I love you so much, sweetheart. Go!"

A single tear slid down my cheek as she whispered she loved me too before running out the front door and slamming it shut behind her.

"You think you can say no to me?" Joel growled, his eyes as dark as pure evil as he squeezed his hands around my throat tightly. I knew I didn't have long before he cut off my air supply and forced me to lose consciousness. I didn't say anything as I continued to squirm, extending my arm as I tried to reach the gun.

"You will never be anything without me! I gave you everything! I did what it took to give you the life you have, the life you deserve! I even went as far as taking care of getting rid of that stupid husband of yours so we could be together!" He let go of my throat and backhanded me across the cheek, the pain immediately stinging my skin.

My eyes snapped to his, processing his words. While we suspected he had something to do with Mike's death after finding everything he left in my apartment, hearing him confirm it made my stomach drop.

"You what?" I asked, my tone changing and softening.

It wasn't that I was happy about what he had done—though it certainly seemed that was how he was taking it. It was the sheer shock of hearing his admission that caught me off guard and drained all the anger from my body.

He pulled back slightly, studying me as he climbed off my body and sat beside me.

"I did what I had to do for us to be together," he said softly, his entire demeanor changing.

"What exactly did you have to do?" I pressed my lips together to keep them from trembling as I attempted to sit up. My entire body ached and hurt in ways I hadn't felt before.

"I took Mike out of the picture."

"How?" My voice cracked as my nose stung from the tears that wanted to spill over.

He waited a few seconds, letting the tension in the room grow thick.

"How!" I screamed, my body beginning to shake with anger.

"I was at the bar that night and paid the bartender to slip something into his drink. When he left, I got in my car and followed him. He was swerving and struggling to stay in his lane, so I gave him a little nudge with my car. It was ridiculous how quickly he lost control of the car and how, even after it flipped that many times, he was still alive when I got out to check on him. All it took was one final blow to the head, and he was out like a light."

My lip trembled as I let him continue talking. I remembered that night so vividly because I hadn't been able to shake the gut feeling telling me he shouldn't go. I didn't want him to mistake my anxiety over something bad happening for me being insecure about him going out with his friends so I didn't say anything. He had gone to the bar with a couple of friends to celebrate a promotion. Shortly after he got to the bar, he texted me to say he wasn't feeling well and was heading home. Mike was never a drinker, so I knew something else had to have happened to make him ill. I never would have guessed that he had been poisoned somehow.

"He begged me to help him. Said that he had a wife and daughter at home that he loved and didn't want to leave. It was almost sad how pathetic he acted. That's what made it so easy to end things for him. You deserved better than that, and I knew I was the man who could give it to you. I was more of a man than he could have ever been. You just needed time to see that."

Knowing this was my only chance, I scooted over, out of his reach, and stood up. It took a few seconds to get my balance, nearly stumbling when I felt his hand grab my ankle. I turned and bent slightly, throwing my elbow down as it made a sickening thud against the side of his head. It was enough to get him to release my ankle as his hands flew to where I'd hit him.

I bent down, grabbed the gun, and fired several shots, not caring which one took his life as his body slumped to the floor and blood puddled around him.

<u>Thirty-Seven</u>
Gage

I was running full steam when we heard another gunshot. It hadn't been that long since the first one, maybe a few minutes if that. But then again, I had lost track of time while focusing on whether Julie was okay, and the cabin seemed a lot further away than I expected. There were several more gunshots fired, sending a chill through me.

"Help! Help!" a little voice cried, pulling my attention to the trees off to the side of the path.

Duke barked, getting to her first as Patrick and I followed him.

"Daisy!" I yelled out, making sure she knew we were there. "Stay where you are, sweetheart. We're coming for you."

"Gage! Mommy needs help!"

"I know, we're on our way. Where are you, sweetie?"

"Here," she cried, her voice getting closer as we went through some brush and saw her sitting on the dirt with her arms wrapped around Duke.

"Baby girl, are you okay?" Patrick asked, swooping down

and picking her up. She wrapped her arms around his neck and cried. He held onto her tightly, as if afraid of what might happen if he let her go.

"Yes. But my mommy…"

"I'm going to go get your mommy now. Stay with Uncle Pat, okay?"

She nodded and held him tightly as he stepped carefully out of the brush and back onto the trail.

"Duke, home," I said, nodding to the inn. While we hadn't practiced much at the inn, I trusted he was smart enough to know what I needed of him right now, given the command was the same as what we used at home.

Once I saw him leading Patrick and Daisy back to the inn, I took off running at full speed until the cabin came into view. I flew around to the front door and pushed it open, stopping when I saw a few people inside.

"Julie!" I yelled, waiting for my eyes to adjust to what was happening in front of me. The room smelled damp and mildewy, likely due to the rundown condition of the cabin that had been abandoned for years. "Julie!"

"This is an active crime scene. You need to leave," a female said, moving to stand in front of me, blocking my view as two males stood off to the side as they shielded a body.

My heart raced in my chest as my blood pressure skyrocketed. Seconds felt like minutes as they ticked by without me knowing whether the woman I was madly in love with was alright. That body on the floor could be hers. There was no way of knowing who fired those gunshots, and worse—who had been killed.

"Julie!" I called again, even louder this time. I looked at the woman standing in front of me, my eyes pleading with her. "Please. I just need to find my girlfri—"

"I'm alright," Julie said quietly, pulling my attention to the corner of the room where she sat in a chair. "Where is Daisy?"

"She's safe. She's with Patrick," I said, stepping toward Julie when the female stepped in front of me again, holding her hand up as she continued to block me.

"I'm not going to tell you again," she warned.

"I'm sorry. I really need to see her and make sure she's okay."

"I understand. However, this is an active crime scene. You cannot be in here. You need to step outside and wait. An ambulance is on the way to check her out, but as far as we can tell, she appears to be okay. We will update you if anything changes." She nodded to the door, indicating it was time for me to go.

I nodded, chewing the side of my cheek to keep from fighting with this woman. Julie and Daisy were okay, so that was all that mattered.

"I'll be outside," I said to Julie, hating that I couldn't go see her yet.

"Okay. I'll be out as soon as I can."

I turned and walked out of the cabin, allowing myself a moment to catch my breath. I had no idea what had happened or whether Julie was truly okay, but she was alive and breathing, and that was good enough for now.

Thirty-Eight
Julie

"I'm fine. Really." I said, exasperated as the paramedic continued to examine the bruises that were already forming on my throat from where Joel had tried to strangle me.

"You need to go to the hospital to get checked out," he said, giving me a pointed look after I had declined the first three times. "You could have internal bleeding, and I'm pretty sure you have a few cracked—if not broken—ribs. It's hard to tell anything without a CT scan. I would feel better if you had a proper assessment at the hospital."

"I need to see my daughter first and make sure she's okay," I said, not wanting to deny medical treatment, but I knew I wouldn't be able to focus on anything until I knew Daisy was okay. While I had seen her for a few minutes when I got to the cabin, I hadn't been able to check on her and had no idea what had happened while she was with Joel.

"Should we take Daisy to get checked out… just in case…" Gage asked, his words trailing off as the paramedic looked between us.

"I don't think it would be a bad idea," I agreed. It had been weighing on my mind for a little while now.

"Where is she?" the paramedic asked after he finished writing his notes down.

"At the inn a few miles down the road. It's on the way to the main road into town," Gage answered.

"We can stop and pick her up on the way to the hospital," the paramedic said. "I'll go let them know. We'll leave in a few minutes."

Once he had walked off, I turned my attention to Gage.

"I don't know if there will be room in the ambulance for all of us," I said softly, not wanting him to feel like he wasn't wanted. "Would you be able to meet us at the hospital? I would really love to have you there with us if you—"

"Absolutely. I'll let Patrick know what's going on and see if he wants to ride over with me."

He walked off, holding the phone to his ear as he let my brother know what was going on.

I breathed out a sigh of relief, thankful for the support we had.

He came back a few minutes later and smiled warmly at me. "It's all taken care of."

"I don't know what I would do without you," I said with a smile as I stared at the man I loved.

"That's something we'll never have to worry about."

He squeezed my hand gently, making a silent promise that only our hearts understood.

****

It was super late by the time we got home from the hospital. Thankfully, everything with Daisy was fine, and they didn't find anything of concern. She told the doctor that Joel had given her a pill to put under her tongue, which made her go to sleep. The doctor assured us that since her vitals were within normal ranges, he felt confident that whatever had been given to her was out of her system. We would continue to monitor her, and if anything out of the ordinary came up, we promised to take her back in.

I, on the other hand, had two cracked ribs and several bruises that hurt like a bitch. But there wasn't any internal bleeding or signs of distress that we needed to worry about. The doctor did suggest that I have someone monitor me during the night, just to be on the safe side, since I'd hit my head so hard on the floor when I fell.

My dad offered to sleep in one of the other rooms so I could sleep in the room with my mom and Daisy. She had been shaken up, and rightfully so, given what happened, so she wanted to be as close to me as possible. While I was in a lot of pain and struggled to get comfortable, we both fell asleep quickly with her tucked in next to me.

By the time I woke up the next morning, my mom and Daisy were already up and in the living room. I climbed out of bed and pulled on a hoodie, a shiver running through me as I looked at the fresh-fallen snow outside. I opened the bedroom door and smiled as I walked down the hall and heard laughter. When I walked into the living room, everyone stopped what they were doing in the living room and stared.

Daisy jumped up and came running over, wrapping her arms around my stomach so tightly that she almost knocked me over. I didn't want to let on to how much pain I was in because her hugs were worth it. I fell to my knees, wrapping my arms around her as I cried. While everything was technically alright, I hadn't been able to stop thinking about everything that had happened.

"I'm so sorry, mommy," she sobbed. "I shouldn't have gone with him at the store. You got hurt because of me."

My heart broke hearing the sadness and worry in her voice. We had talked last night, but it was late, and I didn't want her to stress over everything that happened, so I ended the conversation early. I knew we still needed to talk, but there wasn't a need to rush through it. I wanted to go slow and take things at whatever speed she wanted to move at.

"It's okay, baby. Everything is fine now. It's not your fault. But in the future, please don't do that again."

"I won't. I'm never leaving you ever again."

I hugged her tighter, never wanting to let go.

"Do you think we can let your mommy up so I can fix her some breakfast?" my mom asked Daisy, rubbing her back and smiling at me. "I can't remember the last time your mommy ate a full meal, and we know how important that is."

I started to cry again, feeling the weight of everything as my mom hugged both of us. I was thankful to have my family with me because their support meant more to me than I had ever realized.

"You should eat breakfast," Daisy said, pulling away and wiping my tears for me. "I already ate, so can I keep building my puzzle?"

"Sure," I replied with a soft laugh and a sniffle. "Wait—where did you get a puzzle?"

"About that…" Patrick said, pulling his mouth tight like he always did when he was hiding something. "I might have given her a few things that we picked up at the store yesterday."

"Yeah, me too," Gage replied with an easy laugh.

"We didn't go to the store, but we had stuff we brought as well," my dad said. "Hope you don't mind."

"I don't mind at all," I said with a laugh as I stood up and looked around the room, seeing just how many people loved my daughter.

****

After I finished eating, I sat at the kitchen table and watched as Daisy played a round of Uno with my parents and Patrick in the living room. She knew the rules but had no problem changing them when it came to trying to defeat Uncle Pat. They were having so much fun that I hated the thought that someday soon, this would all end. My parents would go back to Florida. Patrick would return to his busy life in New York. And Daisy and me? I had no clue what we would do or where we would go, which was a bit unsettling.

"How are you doing?" Gage asked as he came and sat beside me, brushing his thumb over my knee as I had them pulled up to my chest.

"I'm okay, I think?" I looked at him and then rested my head on his shoulder to keep him from seeing my tears. "I killed someone."

"I know, baby," he said, wrapping his arms tightly around me. The warmth of his embrace was so soothing that it calmed me in a way nothing else could. "But you did what you had to. If you didn't, he wouldn't have stopped until you were dead."

"I know," I said, my voice trembling. "But I still can't wrap my head around it."

"What I can't wrap my head around is where you got a gun to begin with."

I pulled away slightly and looked at him with a grin.

"I… umm… Well, it turns out that your grandma liked more than shotguns. I found it when I was putting stuff away when Daisy and I first got here. It was in the closet on one of the shelves. I hope you don't mind that I took it."

"That makes sense. That was the bedroom she always stayed in after my grandpa died. I didn't know she had anything other than the shotgun. But I'm glad it came in handy."

"Me too. Your grandma saved the day once again."

"When did she save it the first time?"

"When she opened the inn and created a magical place that made me feel safe." I smiled, the warm memories washing over me.

"I'm glad you came here."

"Me too."

"There's only one problem that we still have to deal with," Gage said, his tone serious.

I shifted slightly so I could see him better. My heart raced as I tried to brace myself for whatever bad news he was about to deliver.

"What's that?"

"I like it here. Coming back, I realized that I don't want to sell it. I want to clean it up and renovate it so I can open it as an inn again. But there's one thing that's keeping me from being able to do that."

My heart fluttered in my chest from the way he was looking at me. I was ready to pretend I was pain-free if it meant getting him alone so he could continue looking at me like that while doing sinful things to my body.

"I don't want to be here and do this if you're not here with me. I want to wake up with you in my arms every morning and go to sleep with you in my bed every night. I want Daisy to binge-watch movies with me while we eat popcorn and she paints my nails. I want a life with you and Daisy more than anything this world has to offer. Would you consider staying here and running the inn with me?"

I gasped as I smiled, my heart filled with more love for this man than I knew what to do with.

"I need to talk to Daisy first," I said, pausing when I saw her head lift as she paused their game to look at us.

"Yes! My answer is yes!" she called, giggling as my mom's head popped up above hers. "But only if Duke gets to sleep in my room."

"Deal," Gage said loudly, smiling as Daisy smiled back at him.

She pulled her arm down in victory while hissing Yes!

"Well, I guess that's settled then," I replied with a laugh. "Our answer is, yes. We would love to stay and help you run the inn."

Thirty-Nine

Julie

Christmas Morning

Soft music played in the living room as Daisy sat in the middle of it, surrounded by a mountain of gifts. Her eyes lit up in pure delight as she stared at them, unsure of where to start. The house was filled with the sweet smell of the cookies we had baked yesterday so we had some ready for when Santa came last night.

Gage had stayed up with me after everyone went to sleep so we could drink the milk and eat the cookie. My dad had written a letter to Daisy from Santa the day that she went missing. That was the reason they hadn't gone into town with us. He had almost forgotten to give it to her until last night, when he suddenly had to check the mail. Her little face was filled with shock and excitement as he read it out loud to her and showed her Santa's signature. That same excitement spilled over into this morning as she practically glowed with happiness.

My mother sat on the couch, watching her as she sipped her coffee beside my dad. Gage and Patrick were on the floor, ready with their tools to free all of her toys from their packaging, and a stack of batteries lined up. I giggled when I saw how serious they were about it, but then I realized that they didn't joke when it came to their love for Daisy.

I had been delayed in getting my shopping done after everything happened with Joel and was starting to stress over it. But I quickly learned that I needed to put one foot in front of the other and focus on small steps, which meant that I agreed to let my parents and Patrick take Daisy into town to do some shopping while Gage and I went off on our own so I could do mine. It wasn't that I didn't trust them to watch her; I was still traumatized over her being taken the first time.

Money didn't feel like an issue anymore, mainly because Gage refused to allow me to pay anything toward the inn or toward the expenses of living there. It would have to be a fight for another day because right now, my focus was on making this the best Christmas ever.

I had bought the most perfect gifts for everyone and couldn't wait for them to open them. I knew that Daisy would love the stuff she got, but I was most excited about the bedroom set Gage and I had picked out for her. The plan was to turn the room she and I had been staying in into her bedroom. They were the only two rooms on that side of the inn, which meant she would always be close to us and not mixed in with the other guests once we started having them.

Daisy ripped open package after package, her excitement growing with each toy she found inside. But when she got to the one with the baby doll she so desperately wanted, that excitement seemed to fade, replaced by sadness.

I leaned forward and set my coffee cup on the table, studying her.

"What's wrong?" I asked, wondering if we somehow picked the wrong doll after all the hassle we went through trying to find the right one in the first place.

"Nothing." She shook her head and kept staring at the baby doll.

"Honey, it's okay. You can tell me. Do you not like her anymore?"

"No. It's not that."

"Is it the wrong one?" Gage asked, rubbing her back soothingly.

"It's the right one. I just remember her being the baby you worked so hard to find before I walked off and left with Joel."

"Oh, baby. It's okay," I assured her as I scooted off the couch and got up to wrap my arms around her. "You don't need to feel bad about that. Everything is okay."

"I know. But I still feel really bad about it. It's all my fault that—"

"No," I replied sternly, moving in front of her as I gently held her chin between my fingers so she would look at me. "None of what happened was your fault. Joel was a very bad man. That had nothing to do with you, sweetie."

She nodded, but I could tell she didn't feel the same happiness she felt a few minutes ago, and I hated that.

"Do you want to open one of my gifts?" I asked, hoping to

change her mood as I raised my eyebrows and grinned.

"Okay," she said with a forced smile.

I ignored the sting I felt in my chest and grabbed the biggest box.

"That's for me?" Her eyes widened as she stared at it.

"Yep. Why don't you open it and see what's inside?"

She grinned big as she tore the paper and gasped when she saw the pink flower comforter and bedding set she had fallen in love with while she was out shopping with my parents.

"This is for me?!"

"It is. We thought you'd like to have your own room now that we'll be living here. We got you a new bed, so we figured you'd need new bedding."

"That's so awesome! Thank you!"

She jumped up and wrapped her arms around my neck, squeezing tightly as her happiness returned. This was all I needed in life: my family and my daughter's happiness.

<u>Forty</u>
Gage

Christmas morning had been fun, but the best part was watching Daisy open her gifts. None of the adults did anything but watch her because her happiness was contagious. By the time she finished, and it was time for us to open ours, we all felt like little kids again. We tore through the wrapping paper and gave the bows to Daisy so she could make something with them, not caring about the mess we made.

After we cleaned up, I helped start dinner preparations, loving how comfortable it felt to have Julie in my kitchen. Lynn guided us through some of the things my grandmother used to do when she hosted Christmas dinner at the inn, and I found myself completely in awe of everything my grandparents did to make this place as magical as it was.

We had shared the news this morning with everyone that we were going to do some remodeling and get the inn up and running again. I had expected to hear how hard it would be and maybe some comments about how I couldn't do it, but what I was met with instead was respect and encouragement.

Julie's parents agreed to stay as long as we would let them so they could help out, which had Daisy beyond excited. There was talk of them selling their condo in Florida so they could move to Silver Falls and be closer to family. Daisy was their only granddaughter, and they both agreed they had missed too much of her life already to miss another day. Before I knew it, Dave was on his phone, looking up information about the abandoned cabins around us.

By the time dinner was ready, the house smelled amazing and reminded me of Christmases spent up here with my family. I smiled as I sat at the head of the table, where my grandfather used to sit, and thanked everyone for being there.

"Does this mean we'll spend Christmas here every year?" Daisy asked as Julie scooped some mashed potatoes onto her plate.

"I don't see why we couldn't," I answered, not wanting to speak for anyone else. "We'll live here, but the invite is always open for you guys to come join us."

"Well, I was looking at a condo in town," Dave said. "It's not too far from here. Maybe half an hour, if that. I was thinking about setting up time to go see it this week."

He nodded proudly as Lynn wrapped her hand over his and gently squeezed it.

"I would love that. I can't wait to move here and be close to our family," she said, smiling at everyone.

An awkward silence fell around the table as everyone waited for Patrick to talk.

"What about you, Uncle Pat?" Daisy asked, putting him on the spot.

He cleared his throat and set his fork down before lifting his eyes to meet hers.

"What would you like for me to do, sweet Daisy?"

"I want you to spend Christmas with us every year!" she cheered loudly, lifting her fork as a few bits of mashed potatoes fell from it.

"What about other holidays?"

"Yes! Those too!"

He pulled his mouth to the side as he nodded, considering something.

"What are you up to?" Julie asked, pointing her fork at him.

"Nothing."

"You're a shitty liar," she continued. "If you're planning to come here for the holidays just to keep an eye on us," she gestured between her and me, "you don't need to bother."

"No. Not everything is about you, Julie," he teased with a playful grin. "Though I'm still debating kicking your ass for dating my sister." He raised an eyebrow at me.

"I'd like to see you try," I said with a snort as I took a sip of my water.

"We'll have plenty of time for that," he replied with a sigh. "I've decided to buy the cabin next door."

He pressed his lips together to keep from smiling as Daisy squealed and dropped her fork.

"For real?!" she exclaimed, eyes wider than a saucer.

"For real," he repeated, grinning at her. "But, there is one condition."

"What's that?" Julie asked.

"I refuse to move here and start a new life while having things in my past left unresolved." He turned to face me. "I'm sorry that I was such an asshole. I should have believed you from the start, and I'm sorry that I ever allowed someone to come between our friendship. While I wasn't thrilled about you and my sister, you've done more than just step up these past few days. You've been there for her—for my family, without any hesitation. Just like you always have. I was an idiot for ever believing anything different about you."

I waited a few seconds before I responded, trying to think about what I wanted to say.

"I'm sorry… that… you were such an idiot," I said, my cheeks burning from how hard I was smiling. "But I forgive you."

"You mother fucker," Patrick said, his chest shaking as he laughed.

"That's not nice," Daisy scolded, looking between us.

"It's okay, sweetheart," I assured her. "It's just how your uncle and I show each other we care. That's what best friends do."

Daisy nodded as if this was good enough for her before she forgot about everything and went about devouring her dinner.

"So that's it?" Julie asked, tilting her head as she stared at her brother. "You're really leaving New York and moving here?"

"I am. Is that okay with you? I guess I should have asked first."

"I love that you'll be so close to us," Julie said, rolling her eyes as she tried to stop the tears. "I didn't realize how much I missed having you guys around until I had to think about you guys leaving. It's like the best gift in the world knowing that you'll all be here with us."

"I wouldn't say it's the best gift just yet," I whispered in her ear as my fingers laced through hers under the table. "I haven't given you my gift yet."

She pulled away as her gaze snapped to mine, a rush of color staining her cheeks.

"Ewww. Gross. Stop it," Patrick said, his face sour as he shook his head and looked down at his plate.

"Better get used to it," I warned as I leaned over and kissed Julie. "Because I don't plan to ever stop loving your sister."

Epilogue
Julie
Eleven-ish Months Later

"The turkey smells amazing," I said as I walked into the kitchen and watched the muscles in Gage's arm flex as he basted it before popping it back into the oven.

"Thank you, my love. But if you keep staring at me like that, no one but me is going to eat this Thanksgiving."

"Because you don't want to share your turkey? What kind of inn are you trying to run?" I teased, chewing my lower lip as his heated gaze collided with mine.

"Because I don't plan to do anything but eat your pussy, and that's not something I will ever share," he replied with a slight growl in his tone.

Fucking hot.

"Do we have time for that?" I asked as he stepped into my space, wrapping his arms around my waist and pulling me against his chest.

"Daisy is at Patrick's, working on a surprise craft project with your mother. They won't be over for an hour, if not later. I don't know what they're doing, but Patrick was bitching about pinecones."

"I vaguely remember him mentioning something about them." I laughed and shook my head.

"You should listen more to what your brother says."

I shrugged my shoulders and tried to fight the grin that threatened to take over as he tickled my sides.

"Ever since he moved here, all he's done is complain about the cold and how Travis tracks everything in the house. I told him not to get a puppy…"

"Yeah, but Daisy was the one who asked for it. You said she couldn't have one here."

"Yep. Just like I said she couldn't bring those pinecones into this house. I know a thing or two about kids and dogs," I teased, scrunching my face.

"Well, I just happen to know a thing or two about multiple orgasms. Why don't we take this conversation to the bedroom and see what else we can learn?" He wiggled his eyebrows playfully as I turned and ran out of the kitchen and down the hall to our room.

I laughed nervously as I felt him behind me, knowing that at any second, he would have me pinned to the bed and doing merciless things to my body. It wasn't that I didn't want him to do those things. I was nervous because he wasn't the only one with something in the oven, and today was the day I was going to share the news with him.

I felt his hands wrap around my waist before they slid up and caressed my breasts, his chest warm and hard against my back. He nudged my head to the side as he kissed my neck, sending shivers across my skin.

"I've been waiting all day to get my hands on you," he whispered in my ear, sending another shiver through me.

"Well, that's disappointing because it's your cock I've been waiting for."

He spun me around, his gaze heated and playful as he arched an eyebrow at me and let his hands fall from my body. I immediately missed his touch.

"Okay, okay," I said with a giggle as I held my hands up. "I like your hands on me, too."

"What else?"

"Your mouth." I chewed my lip as I thought about the other night when he'd made love to me and how I had to keep from screaming so we didn't wake Daisy. But after the third orgasm in a row, it was hard to stay quiet. "God, I fucking love your mouth."

"Well, I love you fucking my mouth. Now, be a good girl and lie on the bed."

I grinned as I tucked my thumbs into my waistband to lower my leggings when he stopped me and shook his head. Instead, he got to his knees and slowly pulled them down as his head lingered right next to my aching pussy. He helped steady me as I stepped out of them, leaving me bare before him.

He licked his lips and grinned devilishly before leaning in and sliding his tongue along my slit.

I gasped and arched my back as my finger gripped his short

hair. He licked again, taking his time teasing me before inserting a finger and fucking me with it.

"Fuck, baby. You're so wet for me," he moaned, pulling away slightly to speak before he leaned in and started sucking my clit while adding a second finger inside of me.

I nodded, my body too aroused and in need of an orgasm to answer him right now.

One hand gripped my ass while the other turned so his fingers hit my G-spot, torturing me in the most beautiful way as stars flashed behind my eyes and I crumbled from one of the best orgasms of my life.

My pussy spasmed as he slowly pulled away and looked up at me, still grinning.

"I planned to eat you on the bed, but this worked too."

"This definitely worked," I agreed with a contented sigh. "But now I need you to fuck me like you do when no one is here so I can be as loud as I want."

"That I can do. Get on the bed, ass up and facing the wall."

I did as he asked, glancing over my shoulder as I heard him pull a condom from the nightstand.

"You don't need it," I said cautiously, pulling my lower lip between my teeth.

He stopped and looked at me, watching me intently as he processed my words. Then his eyebrows shot up on his forehead as he looked from my face to my stomach.

"Are you—?"

I nodded, knowing he couldn't get the word out because I hadn't been able to yet either. I took a test last night when I noticed I was a few days late. I had thought about telling him the news when I found out, but our family was there and I wasn't ready to tell everyone just yet. Plus, we had been busy with all of the food prep for today, so there wasn't much time.

"Fuck, baby. Really?"

I laughed, loving the smile that was on his face as he tossed the condom back in the drawer and walked over to me.

"I'm going to be a dad?"

"You are," I confirmed, the words feeling wonderful to say. "We're having a baby."

"Fuck yeah, we are. I know it's not possible, but I'm going to knock you up again. I want you to have all of my babies."

"Maybe we try one at a time, see how that goes," I teased.

He climbed onto the bed and gave my ass a sharp slap, making me gasp as my pussy ached again.

"Okay. Fine. You can knock me up all you want. Just give me that cock," I moaned as he pressed the tip of it against my entrance while he kissed my neck.

He gripped my hips tightly and slid in, his cock stretching me in the best way. I planted my hands firmly on the bed and let my head hang forward as I popped my ass up, allowing him in deeper. He groaned along with me as he pulled out and then slammed back inside, fucking me hard, the way I loved it.

"I can't believe you're having my baby," he said with a hiss as I clenched around his cock. "Fuck, baby. You're going to make me come if you keep doing that."

"Fuck me harder and I won't make you come just yet."

I knew he was already fucking me as hard as I could handle, but I loved taunting him to see just how much I could get out of him. He reached forward and gently pressed my back forward as he used his knee to nudge my legs open slightly. I rested my face against the mattress and grinned when he fucked me hard and fast, my pussy aching as he hit my G-spot repeatedly until I came, squirting endlessly as he came with me.

I was thankful for many things this year, but sex with Gage was currently at the top of my list—right after my family and good health. There were a lot of new things happening for us with the inn opening soon and a baby on the way, but I knew that as long as I had my family, everything would be alright.

****

Want more Silver Falls? Be sure to grab your copy of Murder and Mistletoe https://books2read.com/u/bz7qjq

Be sure to keep reading for a sneak peek of the first TWO chapters!

Want to come hang out and see what I'm working on? Come find me in my Facebook reader group! https://www.facebook.com/groups/2945710968775398/

Murder and Mistletoe

Samantha Baca

<u>One</u>

Poppy

I grunted as I slammed the shovel into the ground, trying to break through the dirt as a bead of sweat dotted my brow. I looked around to make sure the woods were still as quiet as they were when I dragged the body out here a while ago. It was supposed to be quick and easy—dig a hole big enough to dump his wretched body into, visit my cousin so I had an alibi for being in Silver Falls, and then get the hell out of town. I somehow didn't account for the ground being frozen with a nice layer of snow and ice covering most of it, or how fatigued my body would be after dragging his lifeless body out of the house and shoving him into the car. I was relying on caffeine and adrenaline to keep me going.

I took a deep breath and lifted the shovel again, stopping when I heard the unmistakable sound of footsteps. Panic seizing me as my eyes darted around the forest, trying to pinpoint the direction they were coming from. I didn't have time to run without being caught, and I sure as hell didn't have the luxury of just abandoning the body and pretending I was never there. My footsteps alone would be a good indication that someone was here and that the asshole didn't just come out into the middle of the woods to die the brutal death he had been dealt.

My hands trembled as I tried to focus enough to figure out what to do. The footsteps got louder, and I looked up just in time to lock eyes with the one person I never thought I would see again.

"Poppy?" Patrick asked, stopping a good foot away from me as he took the earbud out of his ear and looked at me. "What are you doing out—"

His words stopped abruptly as he looked from me to the shovel in my hand to the dead body on the ground in front of me.

Fuck.

Two
Patrick

I stepped closer, getting a better look at the man who was hardly recognizable due to the bruising on his face. I lifted my eyes and looked at Poppy, since she was my main concern at the moment.

"What the fuck is going on?" I asked, staring at her as she squirmed beneath my gaze.

"It's not what it looks like," she said, her cheeks flushing red with heat despite the cold air around us.

"Really? Because it looks like you're standing over a dead body and trying to dig up frozen dirt to bury it."

"Okay," she replied softly as she rocked back on her heels. "It's exactly what it looks like."

I shook my head, trying to clear the fog that threatened to take over. I hadn't seen Poppy in at least ten years, maybe longer. She was never close with her family and didn't come around often. I had met her a few times when Gage's family had their reunion at the inn, but she always stayed to herself and was quick to leave as soon as she could.

"Does Gage know you're in town?" I asked, folding my arms over my chest.

She shook her head and looked away.

"Were you planning on telling him?"

"Yeah. I was going to go by and visit before I left."

She looked away from me, and I could tell she was hiding something.

"I'm guessing you didn't come to town just to see him and say hi."

"Nope."

I nodded as all of the pieces started to fall into place.

"What's the deal with the dead guy?"

"He's my husband."

My eyebrows rose involuntarily at the news that she had gotten married. While Poppy didn't keep in touch with her family, I was still surprised no one had mentioned her marriage. Perhaps they didn't know…

"It was a shotgun wedding in Vegas. We were drunk and stupid. He wanted me to be his free use toy. I wanted a divorce. It was our many differences in opinions that led us here." She extended her hands in front of her while holding the shovel under her arm.

"You killed him because he wouldn't give you a divorce?"

"No." Her features sobered as she stared down at him with nothing but rage and fury in her eyes. "I killed him because he was going to kill me."

I noticed the bruises along her neck and the faint bruise on her cheek, which she had tried to cover with makeup. My blood boiled as I continued to stare, taking note of every possible injury on her.

"He tried to kill you." It wasn't a question, just a fact that tasted sour on the tip of my tongue as I said it out loud.

"Several times. We got married six months ago, and my life has been a living hell ever since. I tried to leave so many times, and every time the punishment got worse. A few months ago, I ended up in the ICU because of how badly he hurt me."

"Fuck, Poppy. Did you go to the police and tell them what he did?"

"How could I when he was the sheriff of the small town we lived in? No one would have believed me, Pat. I did what I had to do, and I don't regret it. He won't hurt another woman ever again, so I can live with what I did."

I pressed my lips together and exhaled heavily through my nose. I looked around, making sure we were still by ourselves. There weren't any cabins nearby, which I loved because it was always calm and quiet on my morning runs, unlike what I used to experience when I lived in New York. Minus today, when my morning run was interrupted by finding my best friend's cousin trying to bury her dead husband.

"Give me the shovel," I said, stepping closer and extending my hand to take it.

"What?" she asked, her eyes widening in disbelief.

"The shovel, Poppy. Hand it to me. We don't have much time."

"Pat, you don't have to do this. I don't want to get you caught up in my mess."

"It's a little too late for that. The quicker we can get him in the ground, the better."

She handed me the shovel, and I ignored the spark of electricity that ran through me as our gazes locked again. I'd always been attracted to Poppy, not that I would ever do anything about it. Hell, even if I wanted to, Gage had always made it clear that she was off limits—much like my younger sister, whom he was now dating. But now wasn't the time to worry about any of that as the sun continued to rise, casting a warm glow in the sky above us.

I took a deep breath and let it out, hoping this wouldn't be something I would later regret.

****

Want more Silver Falls? Be sure to grab your copy of Murder and Mistletoe https://books2read.com/u/bz7qjq

Other Books By Samantha Baca

<u>Romantic Suspense</u>

The Haven Brook Series (small town romantic suspense):

'Til Death Do Us Part (Haven Brook Book 1) | The Cradle Will Fall (Haven Brook Book 2) | The Ties That Bind (Haven Brook Book 3) | A Very Haven Christmas (Haven Brook Book 4- Novella) | Three Strikes, You're Gone (Haven Brook Book 5)

The Dark Shadows Trilogy (romantic suspense)

Five Steps Ahead (Dark Shadows Book 1) |Ten Seconds Too Late (Dark Shadows Book 2) | Against The Clock (Dark Shadows Book 3)

Broken (Standalone)

Silver Falls Duet (small town holiday romantic suspense):

Snowed Inn For Christmas | Murder and Mistletoe

Silver Falls Duet (Small town romantic suspense novellas)

Snowed Inn For Christmas | Murder and Mistletoe

Standalone Holiday Novellas

Snow Place To Go | A Very Merry Kissmas | A Christmas Wish | Holiday Hijinks

Standalone Holiday Full Length

Wild Winter

<u>Standalone Books</u>

One Last Wish | Finding Love In Apartment 2C (novella) | Breaking All The Rules (Previously published as: Cocky Counsel: A Hero Club Novel | All Is Fair In Food And War (novella)

Acknowledgments

I'm going to keep these as short and sweet as this book was! Every day that I wake up and am able to write a story is a beautiful day. I'm thankful for the gift of creativity that I've been given, and I hope that those who have taken the time to read this holiday romantic suspense novella enjoyed it!

I couldn't do any of this without my alpha and beta readers. Thank you all for your help! Valerie, Malissa, Claire, Tamara, Amanda, Azucena, Reina, Jackie, Karrie, and Jennifer, you ladies are the best! I appreciate all of your help!

I'd also like to thank all of my ARC readers for diving into this one and leaving those reviews! You have no idea how helpful it is for other readers to find their next great read based on your reviews, so thank you!

As always, I am forever grateful to my family for their constant love and support. My husband and my girls are always there, rooting for me even on days when I feel like giving up. Thanks for not letting me and for pushing me to work harder and do better. I love you all so much!

About the Author

Samantha lives in the southwest with her husband and two children, where she enjoys writing, drinking iced coffee, and watching the greatest show of all time—Friends. With over 30 books published, Samantha enjoys writing across several different genres, from steamy romantic suspense to laugh-out-loud spicy romantic comedies. She also has a sweet spot for holiday stories, so grab a blanket and get ready to binge some of the sweetest—yet spicy—holiday romance your heart can handle!

Samantha loves connecting with her readers, so here's a list of where you can find her:

Facebook Reader Group:

https://www.facebook.com/groups/2945710968775398/

Facebook:

https://www.facebook.com/AuthorSamanthaBaca

Instagram:

https://instagram.com/author_samantha_baca

Webpage:

www.samanthabaca.com

Goodreads:

http://www.goodreads.com/authorsamanthabaca

Books2Read:

https://books2read.com/ap/RQAYK9/Samantha-Baca

www.ingramcontent.com/pod-product-compliance
Lightning Source LLC
Chambersburg PA
CBHW020021310726
48970CB00007B/2151